FRIENDS CLOSE, ENEMIES CLOSER

An IN or OUT Novel

BY CLAUDIA GABEL

IN or OUT

LOVES ME, LOVES ME NOT
An IN or OUT Novel

SWEET AND VICIOUS
An IN or OUT Novel

FRIENDS CLOSE, ENEMIES CLOSER
An IN or OUT Novel

FRIENDS CLOSE ENEMIES CLOSER

An IN or OUT Novel by
CLAUDIA GABEL

Point

For my mother, my first friend

ISBN-13: 978-0-439-91857-2
ISBN-10: 0-439-91857-X

Text design by Steve Scott
The text type was set in Bulmer.

12 11 10 9 8 7 6 5 4 3 2 1 8 9 10 11 12 13/0

Printed in the U.S.A.
First printing, May 2008

Chapter 1

As Marnie Fitzpatrick stood under a stream of water, she looked down at her hands and saw that her fingers were starting to prune. She usually took extra-long showers on Sunday mornings, but never this long. Then again, Marnie had never had a Saturday night as bad as the evening before, so she was hoping that she could prune herself into oblivion. But she knew that in about five more minutes the water temperature was going to leap from lukewarm to bone-chilling cold, which meant the odds of shriveling up into nothingness were slim at best.

Marnie turned the shower off with a slippery wet hand, opened the door, and reached for the plush green towel that was hanging on a hook on the bathroom wall. After she dried off, she wrapped the towel around herself, tucking a small flap of fabric near her chest so it would stay put. Marnie approached the bathroom mirror and wiped off the fog. When she caught her reflection, she practically jumped back in horror.

Oh, my god, what happened to my eyes?

Marnie touched the puffy skin near her eyelids and winced. She figured that they'd swollen up because of the five-hour crying jag she'd had last night after Weston

Briggs had escorted her home from the post inauguration party–fracas. As she grabbed a washcloth and ran tepid water over it in the sink, Marnie felt the tears coming again. She could still hear the pinched, sour voice of that insufferable monster Brynne Callaway, telling her that she was "oh-ver." She could still picture how enraged Marnie's best friend and veritable icon, Lizette Levin, had looked when she accused Marnie of hooking up with skateboard stud Sawyer Lee behind her back. And she could still feel the strong wind that almost knocked her on her butt once Grier Hopkins slammed the door to her exquisite house right in Marnie's face.

As Marnie dabbed the damp washcloth around her blue eyes, her mind was cluttered with angst-ridden questions. Was there a way to convince Lizette that Brynne was a detestable liar who would do anything to see that Marnie bit the dust? Could Marnie hire some-one to run Brynne down with a speeding steamroller? Would she be able to go to school tomorrow and walk the halls knowing that everyone, especially the revered Majors, perceived her to be a dirty, conniving traitor who dared deceive the Almighty Lizette Levin?

Marnie leaned over the sink as her stomach clenched tightly.

I'm screwed. Totally, completely screwed.

"Honey, I'm about to take off," Marnie's mother called from outside the bathroom door.

Marnie had managed to sneak into the house yesterday without running into her mom, so Mrs. Fitzpatrick had no idea that her daughter had been recently punted into the far reaches of the socially ostracized section of the popularity playing field.

"Okay," Marnie replied weakly.

"Do you need anything from the outside world?" her mom asked.

A new life would be nice.

"No, I'm fine." Marnie glanced at her face and saw that she still appeared as though she'd narrowly escaped a dogfight.

"All right, then. I'll just bring Erin straight home after I pick her up from the train station."

A sharp pain shot up from Marnie's stomach and lodged in the back of her head. She had forgotten that her sister would be coming to stay for a while during Penn State's midsemester break. Erin would be there so she could MC the crowning ceremony and distribute tiaras to lucky winners at the Poughkeepsie Central Homecoming dance, among other duties the former senior class queen was expected to perform. How the hell was Marnie supposed to deal with her deity of a sister when a freaking million-ton asteroid had just struck her once-perfect world?

After Marnie heard her mom's Corolla pull out of the driveway, she emerged from the bathroom a soggy, wrinkled mess of a girl. She trudged into her bedroom and threw on a cute pair of purple plaid lounge pants and a ribbed pink tank that she had scored on gojane.com. Putting her wavy blonde hair up in a slick ponytail, she was about to crawl back under the covers and lie there until the dawn of a new civilization. However, her Razr had other ideas. Marnie's heart fluttered for a moment when she heard the Rihanna ringtone, but once she recalled whom that tune belonged to, she wanted nothing more than to throw her cell out the window.

Marnie picked up the call without even saying hello.

"Where's Mom? I've been waiting here for, like, a minute already!" The sound of her sister's squeaky, high-pitched voice was having no trouble exceeding the noisy bustle of the train station.

"She just left," Marnie said, sighing.

"Ugh! Typical," Erin said snottily.

Marnie's jaw had stiffened so much that she wasn't sure she'd be able to utter another word. "Is that all? I have things to do."

"Yeah, right. Oh, and Marnie, my closet better be

just as I left it. Got that?" her sister snapped before hanging up.

Marnie did resort to throwing her phone, but luckily it just hit the mountain of pillows on her bed. No damage done.

Quickly, she made her way down the stairs and into the kitchen, hoping that she could scarf down some food before her mom returned with Erin the Evil. As she rustled through the cupboards in search of a box of Frosted Flakes, Marnie chastised herself for being such a coward. Here she was, scrambling around like a frightened squirrel so she could avoid all contact with her sister and lock herself in her room to mope. This wasn't the same Marnie who had won freshman class treasurer and made out with the most desirable guy in her high school and hobknobbed with the coolest kids in Poughkeepsie's upper echelon. In fact, now that Marnie thought about it, she was acting like . . .

Her perpetually terrified, hive-prone ex-best friend, Nola James. Or at least the version she'd known prior to Nola's metamorphosis into an angry dictator.

Marnie froze when this realization sank in, her eyes fixated on Tony the Tiger's. Thankfully, the *ding-dong* of the doorbell shook her loose of this trance.

She set the box of cereal down on the countertop and scooted across the kitchen linoleum with bare but well-pedicured feet. Marnie opened the door, half-expecting to see the Sunday paper strewn on the porch — the Fitzpatricks had the tardiest delivery person in the neighborhood.

Yet she was standing in front of the aforementioned most desirable guy in her high school, looking as though she'd just crawled out from under a few piles of Sheetrock.

"Hey," Dane Harris said as he pushed up the sleeves of his shirt.

Even though Dane was still as dazzling as ever — his aquamarine eyes sparkling, his cheeks tinged with the slightest bit of pink — he appeared to have camped out at Grier's house. Everything he was wearing was from the evening before and his hair was sort of greasy, as if he hadn't showered yet.

"Hi," Marnie said, swallowing hard.

When she'd returned home from the party, she had tried to get up the nerve to call Dane, explain what happened with Lizette, and swear on three stacks of Bibles that she'd never messed around with Sawyer. (Though she *had* fantasized about it. What girl could blame her?) However, she hadn't been able to stop herself from sobbing long enough to do anything but inhale and exhale.

"Can I come in for a sec?" Dane asked.

Marnie nodded. Right now, Dane was the only person she had left to her decimated name, and she just wasn't sure if she could stand losing him, too.

Dane staggered into the house like he was only half awake — or perhaps he was just sobering up. Marnie had detected a whiff of stale beer on his breath a second ago. Nevertheless, she had never been happier to see him. Marnie closed the door and then led him into her living room.

As Dane flopped down on the beige love seat and put a throw pillow behind his head, Marnie tried to tidy up. Dane had never been inside her house before and if she'd known he was coming over, she would have scoured every inch of the place with the Mr. Clean Magic Eraser and hauled out the old furniture to make way for new pieces from Pottery Barn. Marnie nervously grabbed a bunch of magazines that were lying on the floor and put them on the coffee table. Then she folded a quilt that was haphazardly laid across the recliner, where her father used to doze off while reading *Crime and Punishment*.

Dane patted the empty spot next to him. "Sit down. We need to talk."

Marnie wobbled over to the love seat apprehensively and sat. She was so afraid of what he was going to say that she decided he might change his mind if she beat him to the punch.

"Dane, I know Lizette must have told you why she kicked me out of the party, and I'm sure you're really mad at me, but I —"

"I'm not mad at you, Marnie," he interrupted, his voice steady and calm.

Marnie was stunned. "You're not mad?"

"No, why would I be?"

There's no doubt about it now. Dane is an absolute angel!

"Well, most guys would be angry if they found out that their girlfriend was getting busy with another guy on the sly," Marnie said, her mouth curling up into a soft smile.

Dane was definitely not like most guys.

"First of all, I didn't believe that story for a minute," he said with a smirk.

Marnie wanted to throw herself on top of Dane and cover him in kisses. "You didn't?"

"Of course not," Dane replied confidently. "No girl in her right mind would pick that *scumbag* skater over me."

Suddenly, Marnie felt as though someone had slugged her in the jaw with a two-by-four. Had Dane really said something that awful and arrogant? Maybe she'd contracted some form of rapid hearing loss and had misunderstood him.

"Second of all, you're *not* my girlfriend," Dane added matter-of-factly. "We were just hanging out, know what I mean?"

Now Marnie was certain she'd heard him wrong. *You're not my girlfriend? We were just hanging out?* None of this made any sense to her.

"Actually, I . . . I don't know what you mean." Marnie attempted to stop her voice from trembling. "I thought that since you asked me to the Homecoming dance —"

"That's what I wanted to talk to you about," Dane said, stretching his arms above his head and yawning as though the conversation was boring him. "I can't go to the dance with you anymore."

"Why?" Marnie muttered, willing herself not to cry in front of him.

"Because, even though I don't believe you were fooling around with Sawyer, everyone else who was at that party does," Dane said, looking Marnie right in the eye. "Tomorrow, the entire school will know about it, too. If I don't cut you loose, that would *kill* my rep. I can't let that happen."

Marnie gripped the seat cushion to prevent herself from passing out. Here she'd been worried about Dane dumping her because he thought she'd cheated on him, when in reality all he cared about was his precious image.

He didn't even consider her his *girlfriend* either, so he probably didn't think that he'd just dumped her!

What a grade-A sucker Marnie had turned out to be.

Dane glanced at his freshly polished silver Fossil watch and stood up. "I gotta go." He put his hand on Marnie's shoulder and gave her a look of mock sympathy. "Sorry things turned out this way, but it was fun while it lasted, right?"

When Dane left the room, Marnie buried her flaming-hot face in a throw pillow, silently berating herself for selling out to Lizette, Dane, and all the rest of the Majors.

And for thinking that the fun would last forever.

Chapter 2

As Nola James stood across the street from Marnie's house in her vanilla-cupcake-print pajama pants and bathrobe, she wondered if she'd suffered a brain aneurysm after reading that newspaper article about Matt Heatherly's missing mother. Why else would Nola have dashed over to her ex-friend's place at the first sign of an overwhelming boy-related crisis?

Or maybe it was just a deeply embedded impulse that Nola's body couldn't ignore. Throughout their childhood, Nola had escaped to Marnie's place whenever she was in trouble, so it made sense that instinct would lead her there now. But regardless of the reason, Nola was only twenty-five paces from Marnie's small and somewhat rickety front porch. All she had to do was take a step forward and . . .

What? Have Marnie claw my freaking eyes out?

Nola shook her head in frustration and then spun in the direction of the gigantic Douglas fir that belonged to Marnie's neighbor, Mrs. O'Connor. When Nola and Marnie were little kids, Nola would always hide behind this tree during their marathon games of Girl Hunt, especially on overcast mornings like today. Now all Nola wanted to do was chop it down so she wouldn't be reminded of the great times she and Marnie had shared together. She needed to remind herself of all the rotten things Marnie had done to her since the first day of high school, and how great it had felt to finally dish some well-deserved hurt out to Marnie last week. Apparently there was still a part of Nola that was holding on to the idea of Marnie as her soul sister, and if Nola wasn't careful, she might wind up . . .

"My, oh my," came a voice out of nowhere.

Nola hoped that somehow, Marnie's street had been rezoned into the Land of Oz, and Mrs. O'Connor's fir tree was speaking to her. But when Nola turned around slowly and saw that Dane Harris was gawking at her impishly, a sour taste spread throughout her mouth.

"I *love* your new look, Mrs. Billingsworth." Dane scratched behind his right ear and half-grinned as he took Nola in from the top of her messy bun to the bottom of her Skechers. "But if you lost the robe, you'd be even sexier."

Nola glanced down and noticed that her robe had opened up and exposed her somewhat-sheer and a-tad-too-clingy-for-outdoor-use heather-gray tank top. Dane's gaze settled on her chest, which caused Nola to whip back around to face the fir tree and retie her robe so that the collar came up to her neck.

Dane laughed as he came in close behind her and whispered in her ear, "Aw, Marnie told me you could be painfully shy around guys. What did she call it? Oh yeah. 'Boy-related asthma'!"

Nola felt as though someone had poured lighter fluid all over her and thrown a lit match at her feet. Was Marnie absolutely incapable of keeping *anything* to herself? It seemed like every member of the male persuasion who sucked face with Marnie ended up knowing something private about Nola!

Dane trotted in front of Nola and grinned at her. "Are you having trouble breathing? I'm certified in CPR, you know."

Nola's eyes grew wide with scorn as her heart raced furiously. "Actually, I'm having trouble preventing myself from *wringing your neck*!"

"There's the Mrs. Billingsworth I've come to adore," Dane said, raucously clapping his hands as though he were being entertained.

Nola grunted and pushed Dane aside forcefully so she could storm down the street. However, it seemed like shoving him only provoked Dane more.

"C'mon, don't leave," he said, trying to keep up with a near-sprinting Nola. "I was just kidding around."

Nola let out a bitter "Ha!"

"I really like aggravating you. I can't help it," Dane continued while Nola quickened her pace. She would have turned the corner, too, if he hadn't grabbed her wrist.

"Let go of me, you —"

"Preptard?" Dane said with a smirk. "I never forget a good diss."

Nola willed herself not to crack even the slightest hint of a smile, but her efforts were futile. Calling Dane that ridiculous name a couple weeks ago was one of her finer moments in the comeback category.

"I'll let go if you listen to me for ten seconds. Deal?"

Nola tried to disregard the fluttering sensation inside her tummy as Dane's skin touched hers. "Make it eight seconds."

"Obviously something's wrong, or else you wouldn't be standing outside of Marnie's house looking like a desperate housewife. Are you all right?"

Nola's brow furrowed. Where was this concern coming from? And was it even real? Dane always seemed just as hollow and self-centered as Lizette and the rest of the Major crew. Was he just reeling her in so he could turn around and ridicule her?

"I'm fine, I just —" Nola stopped herself. Giving Dane any hints about why she was there would be social suicide. He'd make sure everyone at school knew how much she cared about Matt. Though there was a good chance people suspected as much at this point, especially with that rumor Marnie had started about Nola and Matt in English class a few days ago.

"Just what?" Dane asked, loosening his grip on Nola. "Seriously, if there's something the matter, you can tell me."

Nola searched Dane's bright eyes for any indication that he might be sincere and/or human. There was some friendliness in them, but only a glint, though. Still, she needed to figure out what to do about Matt right away, and that was much more important. Nola peered back down the street toward Marnie's house and saw that there wasn't a car in the driveway. Perhaps Dane was her one shot at getting to Matt's house on Ridge Road. Maybe she'd have to put her trust in the Vice President of Smarmy for the greater good.

Besides, when Nola realized that she hadn't even brought any money for the city bus, she figured her transportation options were limited. There was absolutely no way she was getting into the family Forester with her dad and her little brothers. The last thing she needed was to show up at Matt's house with huge welts on her arms from wrestling with Dennis and Dylan in the backseat.

"I just need a ride," Nola mumbled.

"Oh, I'll give you *a ride*." Dane snickered.

God, I despise this jerk!

Nola broke free of Dane's grasp, but before she could march off in a rage, Dane put his arms around her in what seemed like a tight hug.

"Wait! I'll take you wherever you want to go! I promise I won't be a skeeze anymore!" he pleaded. "Really, I want to help!"

"Fine! Just back off, will you?" Nola said, squirming.

Immediately Dane released Nola and withdrew. "Sorry, sorry. I don't know what came over me."

Nola rolled her eyes. "Yeah, right."

"Stay here, and I'll go get the car, okay?"

Nola crossed her arms over her chest and shrugged.

As Dane jogged a few yards away to a shiny Jaguar convertible, Nola wondered why she was agreeing to accept any kind of favor from Marnie's weasel of a boyfriend. But the moment Nola looked at the newspaper ink that had stained the tips of her fingers, she knew that when it came to Matt Heatherly, she'd do just about anything.

Nola followed Dane to the car, got in, and put on her seat belt. Dane leaned over Nola, flipped down the passenger-seat visor, and snagged a pair of dark-tinted

Oakley sunglasses (even though the sky was littered with clouds).

"Where to?" he asked as he started up the Jag's V-6 engine.

"Ridge Road," Nola said.

Dane stomped on the gas and peeled out. "Cool, huh?"

"Not so much," she replied, tensely.

While Dane careened through town, Nola looked out the window and thought about what she was going to say to Matt now that she knew about his mother. But when the car hit a large construction zone that closed off a lane, Nola was forced to engage in mindless conversation with Dane.

"So, are we going to your *boyfriend's* house?" Dane said, tapping his hands on the steering wheel as they sat still in traffic.

"*We* aren't going anywhere," Nola snapped. "And my destination is *none of your business*."

Dane snickered while wiping off his sunglasses with a microfiber cloth. "Aw, you're embarrassed about your Sunday-morning booty call. Isn't that precious?"

Nola craned her neck so she could see if the tall construction worker in the distance had put down his red STOP sign and held up a yellow SLOW sign, but no luck.

“That’s funny, coming from Vice President Booty Call himself.”

“*Au contraire, mon frère.* I was at Marnie’s place to break up with her, not hook up with her.”

“Huuuuuuh?!” Nola said, totally astonished.

“She took it like a champ, though. Gotta give the girl props for that.”

“What happened?”

“None of your business.” Dane smirked. “Besides, I’m sure you’ll hear about it through the PoCen grapevine, like everyone else.”

UGH! Why can’t a bolt of lightning strike this jackass?

Suddenly, the Jag accelerated a bit and then came to a screeching halt, causing Dane and Nola to jerk forward. Nola steadied herself by putting her hands on the dashboard and stretching her legs out.

“Sorry,” Dane said. “I haven’t had my morning cappuccino yet.”

Nola rolled her eyes and leaned back in her seat, when she felt something roll underneath her right Skecher. She picked her foot up and saw a familiar handmade bracelet on the floor mat. Nola removed her seat belt so she could reach forward and grab it. When the bracelet came into view, Nola smiled — even covered in dirt, it looked as pretty as it did the day she’d made it for Marnie.

However, as she ran her fingers along the strands of beads, the first person that popped into Nola's mind was her brothers' babysitter, Ian Capshaw. The bracelet must have jogged Nola's memory of his delicious rouge lips because she and Ian had been searching for mishandled necklace beads in her bedroom carpet when they became "sidetracked." The vivid mental picture was enough to make Nola woozy.

"What do you have there?" Dane asked curiously.

Nola was too overwhelmed to answer, so she just held the bracelet out in the palm of her hand.

"Oh, Lizette must have left that behind last —" Dane cut himself off abruptly, his cheeks turning bright pink.

Nola's eyebrows arched. Had Dane just let a juicy piece of info slip?

Unfortunately, the yellow SLOW sign appeared, which meant that Nola wouldn't be able to hear the ending to this suspicious sentence.

"Thank god, we can finally move." Dane shifted the Jag into first gear.

As he maneuvered around the construction area and out of traffic, Nola put the bracelet into her robe pocket for safekeeping. Dane didn't seem to notice, nor did he say another word on the way to Ridge Road. When he left Nola off in front of Matt's house, Dane just said,

"See ya later, Mrs. B," and sped down the road like he was trying to outrun something.

Nola patted the outside of her pocket as she watched Dane's Jag take a sharp corner. This bracelet was definitely the key to unlocking an ugly secret. If Nola decided to give it back to Marnie and reveal where she had found it, sizable shock waves would rock her ex-best friend's life. But Nola couldn't think about that right now. She had to help a temporary best friend face an ugly secret of his own.

Chapter 3

REASONS TO LIVE, AN ABRIDGED LIST

1) College — I can move across the country and start over at some posh university like Stanford! All I have to do is get through four more lousy years at PoCen and save up forty grand for first year's tuition. (Defeated sigh)
2) I think the new season of The Hills will be out on DVD. That might bring me some tiny fraction of joy.
3) My mom's double chocolate walnut brownies. She just baked a batch and they are DEEE-LISH! (But I ate ~~five~~ six of them, and don't feel like going running. That's a recipe for thunder thighs, isn't it?)
4) Being freshman class treasurer. Oh wait. Without Dane and Zee, that's going to suck with a vengeance now. (Defeated sigh squared).
5) God, what's the use?

Marnie took a long gulp of ice-cold two-percent milk after finishing her sixth brownie and wiped the dribble off her chin with the bottom of her shirt. She was sprawled out on her bed, her thick Martha Stewart brand comforter wrapped around her legs and a stack of squishy pillows behind her back, propping her up. A string of melancholy emo-tunes filled her room and tugged on the last remaining string of her heart. Marnie couldn't believe how terrible she felt, and the brownies she'd consumed weren't helping.

However, when Marnie heard her mom's car pull into the driveway, she felt much worse — kind of like she'd been shot in the kneecaps with an air rifle.

Erin Fitzpatrick, Poughkeepsie Central High School legend and irrefutable pain in the ass, had returned from Penn State.

Marnie's bedroom window was opened a crack so she was able to listen to her sister and her mother talk as they approached the house. Marnie's mom was always doting on Erin, as though her older daughter had been born covered in glitter.

"It's so good to have you back, sweetie," Mrs. Fitzgerald said cheerily. "The house just hasn't been the same without you."

Marnie rolled her eyes, but her mom was right. The house had actually been far less crowded without Erin's stuff everywhere, and the atmosphere was a lot more enjoyable without Erin being in close proximity. At least that was how Marnie saw it.

"Well, I hope you don't expect me to have a curfew while I'm home," Marnie heard her sister snip. "I'm, like, a grown woman now."

Oh PLEASE! Erin is the biggest overgrown child in North America!

"We can certainly talk about it. I know you're going to be very busy reconnecting with all your friends, my little social butterfly," her mom cooed.

Marnie's indigestion and busted kneecaps had suddenly been upgraded from fair to critical condition.

She yanked her comforter over her head once she realized Erin and her mom had crossed the threshold into their house. In the warm darkness beneath the covers, Marnie wished that her father had fixed the lock on her bedroom door before he had moved to Connecticut, but what was the point of wishing for things that would only delay the inevitable? Marnie would have to come out of her room sometime, and when she did, she'd have to confront the frostiness in Erin's turquoise eyes.

Without warning, a petite but freakishly strong hand yanked Marnie's comforter off of her. If she hadn't clung to her matching Martha sheets, Marnie would have been practically thrown onto the floor.

"Aren't you going to help me bring in my bags?" Erin glowered as she stood over Marnie like a giant stick figure in snakeskin spiked heels.

Even though Marnie was not even remotely happy to see her sister, she couldn't get over how fantastic Erin looked. Her sleek waist-length blonde hair was ultra Gwyneth and catching so much sunlight it nearly blinded Marnie. Her eyebrows were plucked into a perfect arch and her makeup was flawless. She was wearing a strawberry-red stretch poplin dress, cinched with a violet-colored rough-hewn belt. If Lizette Levin were there, she surely would have said that Erin was absolutely, positively boss.

"Can't you see that I'm busy?" Marnie said, wrenching the comforter out of Erin's hands.

"Yeah, busy being *lazy*," Erin replied with a snarl.

Marnie picked up the alarm clock on her nightstand and held it to Erin's face. "Wow, you've been in my room for ten seconds and I already want to drop-kick you! That has to be a new record."

Erin traipsed across the room like she was strutting down a catwalk and stopped in front of Marnie's vanity mirror so she could check out her reflection. "I guess I'll make myself comfortable, then," she said.

Why, God, why?

"So, did you mess things up with Lizette or what?" Erin took a moment to peek at a strip of black-and-white photos that was tucked into the mirror frame where a picture of Marnie and Nola used to be.

Marnie and Lizette had taken those shots in a booth at the Galleria after one of their massive shopping sprees. In one picture, Marnie was touching her tongue to her nose (a talent she had previously only showcased in front of Nola) and Lizette was crossing her eyes and laughing. Another picture featured Marnie and Lizette smiling with their arms around each other. Marnie's neck stiffened at the thought of not making any more fun memories with Lizette. And at the thought of explaining what had gone down to her sister.

Even so, it didn't make any sense for Marnie to lie to Erin. News traveled lightning-fast in their school and since Erin was considered the be-all-end-all by each and every teenage citizen of Poughkeepsie, her sister would find out about the blitzkrieg with Lizette by the time she unpacked.

"Let's see," Marnie said. "I followed your dumb advice and kissed Brynne's behind until my lips fell off. Then, whaddya know, she double-crossed me anyway! So now Zee hates me and by tomorrow morning, everyone at school will think I'm a total loser."

Marnie could see her sister's mouth break into an amused smirk in the mirror. But Erin caught herself quickly, and when she turned around, she was stone-faced. "My advice *wasn't* dumb. Anyway, you still have that hottie Dane in your pocket. He'll keep you afloat with all the Majors until Lizette chills out."

Marnie immediately felt that shaky sensation she always got before she started crying. She tried to think of a way to stop herself from breaking down, but when she attempted to adjust her posture or perform the yoga breathing that she'd learned, her eyes began to glisten with tears.

"Dane came over earlier and —"

"He didn't ditch you, did he?" Erin's worried expression led Marnie to believe this was more terrible than being in a mammoth fight with Lizette.

Marnie nodded at her sister. She knew if she tried to speak, the sobbing would commence.

"Ugh, this is just what *I* need," Erin proclaimed as she threw her hands up in frustration. "Stupid crap to ruin Homecoming for me."

Marnie shouldn't have been surprised by Erin's self-centered response, but she was. Surprised and furious. So furious that instead of being on the verge of crying, she was now on the verge of pouncing on Erin, fangs unleashed. "Wait a minute. *My* life is in shambles and *you're* pissed off?"

"Don't you get it? Everyone will be gossiping about how my pathetic little sister was booted from the Majors. No one will be talking about what really counts." Then Erin pointed at herself. "*Me!*"

Marnie's rage gave way to a small sense of satisfaction. Erin was upset that she was going to lose some of her beloved spotlight to her younger sister. That had never, *ever* happened before. Marnie hadn't been in the position to really pose a threat to Erin's fabulousness, and while she'd rather not be the source of negative gossip, a wise person had once said that any publicity was good publicity.

"Better get used to it, sis. I made it into the Majors in less than a month," Marnie said, mustering up as much courage as she could. "And I may be down for now, but I'm certainly not out."

After an angry grumble, Erin spun around and strode out the door, her long shimmering hair cascading behind her.

As for Marnie, all that was left for her to do was believe in what she'd just said.

Chapter 4

"Oh, my god, Nola. What are you doing here?"

This wasn't exactly the greeting Nola had expected to receive when Dane dropped her off at Matt's place unannounced on the morning the *Poughkeepsie Journal* had spilled the Heatherly family's secrets. Nor had she expected Matt to look so unbelievably gorgeous, even though it was quite obvious he had been crying. While his eyes were red and the corners of his nose appeared as though they had been rubbed raw with Kleenex, Matt's lips were the color of an azalea and his shaggy brown hair skimmed the top of his perfect ears. She could just stand there until the end of time, gaping at him.

"Are you going to answer me or stand there like a garden gnome?" Matt asked, crossing his arms over his chest so his toned biceps flexed a bit.

"I'm sorry, I know I should have called first but —" Nola took in a deep breath. "I left my house in a rush."

A smile crept across Matt's face. "I can see that."

Nola glanced down at her robe to make sure it was still tied tight. A light mist of rain had started to fall the second she knocked on Matt's door, and a brisk chill was in the air. She didn't want Matt to catch a glimpse of her goose bumps (which Nola suspected weren't really due to the climate).

"Can I come in? I kind of need to talk to you."

"Yeah, my dad just went on a Home Depot run. We can hang out in my room."

Nola noticed how the drawstring of Matt's maroon Epic soccer shorts was coming undone and wondered if going up to his bedroom would be a good idea. What if, in a moment of weakness, she threw herself at Matt like a very cheap imitation of his supah-fly girlfriend Riley Finnegan (whom he'd probably already gotten to third base with)?

Quickly, Nola steadied herself. Now was definitely not the time to be obsessing over Matt's rockin' body or his relationship with Riley. Matt was hurting badly, and she had to be there for him as a friend, regardless of how much she wanted him to be more.

Matt led Nola into his house, which was in a complete state of disarray. There were clothes scattered around the living room along with a few opened bags of potato chips on the couch and the floor. As Nola and Matt went up the stairs, she saw a stack of empty Coors Light bottles near the recycling bin in the kitchen. Nola swallowed hard. What if Matt's father was drinking too much? And then a new thought occurred to her — with the amount of time his dad spent away from home, Matt could be drinking, too.

Not that she could really blame either of them after what she'd read this morning.

Matt shoved open the door to his bedroom. The same type of messy clutter that Nola had observed downstairs wasn't in his room at all. In fact, it looked like Matt had cleaned and reorganized since the last time she'd been here. Nola breathed a sigh of relief. Maybe Matt wasn't in as much despair as she had thought.

"So have a seat," Matt said, gesturing to his hospital-corners-made bed.

Nola plopped down on the edge, grabbing Matt's pillow nervously and holding it in her lap. She had no idea how she was going to approach the subject of Matt's mother. Should she just come straight out and say that she read the article, or give him a few hints that would lead him where she wanted to go?

However, when Matt sidled up next to Nola so that one of his legs was touching hers, she blurted out:

"I'm sorry that I flicked your ear!"

Matt stifled a laugh. "Thanks for coming all this way to tell me that, Nola. But I've got bigger things on my mind."

Slowly, Nola took one of her hands off the pillow and put it on Matt's. "I know. I saw the article this morning."

Suddenly, Matt's head bobbed forward so his chin almost touched his chest and his shoulders shook. Nola looked on worriedly as tears streaked his face — she wasn't sure how to console him.

"I wanted to tell you, Nola. I really did," Matt said, sniffling. "But then I realized that I *liked* you not knowing about all that stuff."

Nola was confused. Matt wanted to keep her in the dark about something this important? "I don't understand."

Matt looked up at Nola and wiped at his eyes with his hands. "When I was with you, I could be in this world where my past wasn't following me around. I could finally allow myself to be happy without carrying all this crappy baggage with me. I guess it just made our relationship sort of . . . sacred. Does that make any sense?"

Nola had never wanted to hold Matt in her arms more than she did right then. "It makes a lot of sense."

Matt flashed a weak grin and then took her hand in his. "I really appreciate you coming over."

"Not a problem." Nola could feel a flash of burning heat scorch her neck, but she didn't care if she broke out in hives. "And you don't have to talk about your mom if you don't want to."

"Actually, I would like to talk about her, if you don't mind," Matt replied, his voice cracking a little.

"That's why I'm here," Nola said as she wrapped her other hand around Matt's.

All of a sudden, Matt jerked away. "Hold on a sec, Nol. My phone is vibrating."

Damn. It. To. HELL!

Matt stood up and fished out his cell phone from the pocket of his soccer shorts. He flipped it open and peered at the screen. He seemed bewildered, like he was deliberating whether or not to pick up the call. After a few tense seconds, he shut his phone and sat back down on the bed next to Nola.

"That was Riley. I'll just call her back later," Matt said.

Nola almost threw her arms up in a victory pose.

"So what was I saying before we were interrupted?"

You were madly in love with me and wanted to kiss me all over?

"That you wanted to talk about your mom," Nola said, scratching at the bottom of her neck.

Matt gazed at her with concern. "Hives again?"

"I've got a secret, too," Nola said, grinning. "I always get them when I'm nervous."

Matt squatted in front of her so she could stare into his beautiful hazel eyes. "I can't believe you never told me that."

Nola shrugged.

If he only knew what else I haven't told him . . .

"Well, you shouldn't be nervous. It's just me." Matt leaned forward and touched his forehead against hers. "Capisce?"

"Uh-huh," was all Nola could mutter.

"Good." Matt stood up again. "So, do you want to see a picture of my mom?"

Nola shook herself out of her stupor. "Yes, I'd like that."

Matt ambled over to his dresser and picked up the photograph that Nola had spotted behind a slew of CD jewel cases the first time she set foot in Matt's room. He brought it over to Nola and handed it to her gingerly.

Nola always thought Matt resembled his father quite a bit, but now that she was staring at a photo of his mother, she could see all the physical traits they shared. For instance, Matt's ears stuck out a tiny bit at the top, just like his mom. Matt had inherited the flecks of amber highlights in his hair from her, too. But then as Nola studied Mrs. Heatherly's face, she noticed the qualities that made her unique and special — the freckles that covered the bridge of her nose, the rounded shape of her jaw, and the full lips that were stained ruby red.

"She was so pretty," Nola said.

"She *is* pretty," Matt said, his tone upbeat. "I haven't given up hope that she's still out there, waiting to be rescued."

"Hope is always a good thing," she said, looking at the sunny expression on Mrs. Heatherly's face.

"There have been times when it hasn't been, Nol." Matt sighed. "The first month that my mom was gone, I cut school all the time and searched for her on my bike. Even after we packed up and moved here, I did the same thing. Just rode around aimlessly on streets I didn't know, hoping that I'd find her somehow."

Nola felt a shiver travel down from her chest and into her legs.

"I was suspended from Arlington for three days when I picked up a ton of absences, but at least the principal kept the reason quiet, out of respect for my family's privacy, of course."

Thankfully, Nola was able to prevent herself from gasping out loud. Even so, she was still pretty stunned. All this time, Nola had thought that Matt's suspension from school was linked to some grade-A derelict past. In reality, though, Matt had been penalized for skipping school so that he could search for his missing mom.

Nola didn't think she could feel even more strongly for Matt, but she was glad he'd proven her dead wrong.

"And then at some point, I just stopped looking," Matt mumbled. "I don't even know when or why. But I stopped."

Quietly, Nola got off the bed, setting the picture on the pillow that she'd been anxiously strangling only a few minutes earlier. Then without hesitating or fearing how Matt would respond to the gesture, Nola slipped her arms around his waist and wrapped him in a warm, close hug.

"You've never given up in your heart, Matt," she whispered. "That's all that matters."

When Nola felt Matt's arms travel up her back and his head rest on her shoulder, she knew what she'd just told him was undeniably true.

Sunday, October 14, 10:48 P.M.

queenzee: *i want my graphic print tory burch minidress back*
queenzee: *TOMORROW*
marniebird: *zee! please, PLEASE listen*
queenzee: *2 what? more LIES?*
marniebird: *i've never lied 2 u, i swear*
queenzee: *plz. i suspected u & sawyer all along, ever since that football game*
marniebird: *NOTHING happened between us!!! brynne is lying!!!*
queenzee: *whatev, i can't believe i WASTED my time on u*
marniebird: *what can i do 2 make things right, zee?*
queenzee: *just give me my dress and then stay away from me. GOT IT?!*

queenzee signed off at 10:50 P.M.

Chapter 5

On Monday morning, Marnie tried to relax in the passenger seat of her mother's Corolla while her sister drove with one eye on the road and the other eye on her reflection in the rearview mirror. Marnie shook out her legs, which were looking nice and toned in her opaque burgundy tights. She stretched out her arms in front of her and loosened up the muscles in her shoulders. But every time Marnie found a tiny shred of serenity, Erin managed to chew it to pieces by cutting off other cars with barely an inch to spare between bumpers.

In fact, Erin swerved and passed a businesswoman who was parallel-parking her VW Bug with such speed that Marnie's seat belt couldn't prevent her from smacking into the car door.

"OW!" Marnie cried out, rubbing her elbow. If it wasn't for her chunky cream-colored karate belt sweater, she probably would have broken a bone.

"Sorry." Erin slammed her dainty hand on the horn and honked at the vehicle in front of her.

"God, Erin. The light just turned green!" Marnie slunk down in her seat, embarrassed. "Why are you driving like a crazy person?"

Erin grabbed Marnie's bag off of her lap and rifled through it with one hand. Once she located Marnie's molten-brown peach-blossom gloss, Erin started reapplying the honey-colored shimmering liquid to her lips. "I don't want you to be late for school, that's all."

"You're just in a hot sweat to meet the Homecoming planning committee and show off your fake pageant wave," Marnie scoffed.

"Envious, are we?" Erin tossed Marnie's tote onto the car floor.

"Gimme a freaking break," Marnie said under her breath.

The truth was, Marnie wished that all the anger, anxiety, desperation, and worry that were bubbling up inside of her had everything to do with her sister's return to Poughkeepsie and nothing else. At least then Marnie could expect to walk through the halls at school and find her best friend, Lizette, waiting by her locker and wearing some divinely inspired outfit that would make Marnie smile.

However, when Erin pulled into the visitors' parking lot, Marnie was struck by the harsh reality of her situation. As of today, the Almighty Lizette Levin was not her friend anymore.

How did I ever get myself into this hot steaming mess?

Erin craned her swanlike neck back and tossed her hair as she backed the Corolla into an empty space. Then out of the blue, she slammed on the brakes and shrieked. Marnie turned around just in time to see her sister narrowly miss hitting a boy on a skateboard. Marnie locked eyes with him, and her heart leaped into her throat.

Sawyer Lee.

Marnie hadn't seen Sawyer since she'd insulted him the other day, at Lizette's scornful urging. He appeared very startled, which seemed appropriate considering that he'd almost been flattened by a few tons of steel. But at the same time, Sawyer was still the epitome of laid-back cool. His buzzed hair brought out the striking angles of his face, and his black eyes gleamed at Marnie as she soaked up the rest of him — loose-fitting brown plaid pants that flared over his Vans and a red Krooked shirt.

Marnie opened her mouth as if she was going to apologize for her behavior. But Sawyer's eyes had already cast themselves down to his feet. He hopped back onto his board and glided off before she could even get out of the car.

"Those skater turds *never* look where they're going," Erin said, fanning her glistening cheek with a shaky hand.

Marnie practically kicked open the door with her light camel, western–style stitch-worked boots. "Sawyer is *not* a turd."

Erin exited the Corolla gracefully. "*That's* Sawyer Lee? As in Lizette's ex-boyfriend?"

Marnie wanted to ignore Erin entirely. But there was absolutely no one on her side now, not even Dane. That meant Erin was the only person she could turn to, even if her advice was pretty useless.

"Yeah, that's him," Marnie admitted, her voice low and sheepish.

Erin stood on tiptoes so she could get a better look at Sawyer, who was performing nosegrinds off the curb with a couple of his friends. "I can see why she's pissed that you stole him. He's a total *hawt dawg*."

Marnie groaned. "I didn't *steal* him. *He* broke up with *her*! And Sawyer and I didn't do anything but *talk*!"

"Little sis, what you *say* doesn't matter anymore. It's what you *do* that counts," Erin crowed as she put her fingers through the belt loops of her shapely Diesel jeans.

"Fine. What should I *do*, then?

"First of all, you need to avoid Sawyer like he's a homeless man begging for money, and trashtalk him behind his back whenever you can."

Marnie's face crinkled into a baffled expression. What was that going to accomplish?

"You have to show Lizette that you're not into him."

But I've always been into him. Marnie knew better than to say that out loud.

"Second of all, you should go out with another guy. Anyone will do." Erin bent over and adjusted a strap on her black suede shoes. "Again, this will prove to Lizette that you don't like Sawyer and, eventually, she'll stop being such a big drama mama."

Marnie couldn't help but snicker. Erin was the Commander in Chief of Drama Mamas!

"Third of all, and this you *have* to remember," her sister said, flipping back up so fast that her boobs bounced in her snug garnet-colored wrap top. "Keep your friends close and your enemies closer."

As Marnie let those words seep in, Erin went into shriek mode again. Former members of last year's Homecoming court dashed at them from all directions and swarmed Erin in a giant spastic hug. It was then that Marnie realized the only people she had to keep close were enemies, and the last remaining fragment of courage she'd had crumbled inside of her.

As Marnie strolled down the halls of Poughkeepsie Central alone, clutching her bag as though it were a can of pepper spray, she tried to keep her chin up and cast her eyes straight ahead of her. But whenever a girl peered at her and giggled mischievously, or a boy pointed at her and chuckled, Marnie's head drooped and her shoulders hunched forward so no one could see her face.

God, this is worse than I thought.

However, when Marnie took a glimpse at her locker and saw Lizette blocking it like an angry pit bull, she knew things were about to go from worse to Lord-have-mercy-on-your-pitiful-soul.

Lizette's cheerful outfit didn't match her scowl though. She had paired a plaid straight-cut suit jacket with a canary-yellow chiffon tunic dress and hot-pink opaque tights. She looked as though she were going to appear on a children's television show rather than bite into Marnie's neck and tear out a major artery or two.

Marnie inhaled deeply and stood motionless in front of Lizette, who was chomping hard on a piece of tropical-flavored gum and impatiently tapping her emerald-green peep-toe slingbacks on the floor. Even though she was willing herself to stay composed and poised, a part of Marnie wanted to fall to her knees and beg Lizette for a second chance, even if she hadn't done anything wrong.

"Hi, Zee," Marnie said meekly, hoping that her warm smile would cut through the thick block of ice that was surrounding Lizette.

"Do you have my dress?" Lizette snipped.

Marnie reached into her bag and pulled out the Tory Burch mini. "Thank you again for loaning it to me." Her voice was teetering on the edge of tears.

Lizette snatched it out of Marnie's hand as though she were a lioness pawing at an annoying fly. She held the dress up in the air and began inspecting it thoroughly. Then Lizette's face contorted into what could only be described as revulsion.

"How disgusting!" Lizette shouted. She turned and cupped a hand around her mouth for maximum volume. "Guys, come here! You have to see what Marnie did to *my* Tory Burch!"

Marnie's heart collapsed as Brynne and Grier responded to Lizette's summons and sauntered over from their lockers. As per usual, Brynne was oozing out of a zebra-print jersey dress while Grier pitter-pattered down the hall in a cable-knit sweater and a crisp pencil skirt.

Whatever they were going to do to her, Marnie wished it would be over with quickly. People were still ambling around in the hall, making their way to homeroom.

Brynne gaped at the dress, which Lizette held out way in front of her as though it were radioactive. She grinned devilishly so the space in between her teeth showed. "Ohmigod! Are those *armpit stains*?"

Grier squinted at the dress and then her eyes grew wide. "Ew, they are!" she said, shuddering.

As for Marnie, she wanted to fast-forward the clock to three P.M.

Lizette dangled the dress close to her nose and sniffed it. "Gross, it smells like BO, too."

"Ick, that's wicked nasty," Brynne said, and pinched her nostrils shut.

Marnie couldn't believe what she was seeing or hearing. She hadn't even *worn* the dress. And she had even sprayed it with Febreze and ironed it last night. The dress was in picture-perfect condition! Sure, she expected these crude lies from Brynne, but why was Lizette acting so heinously? Was she really that upset over a boy? True, this was no ordinary boy — this was the incredible Sawyer Lee — but it still seemed bizarre that Lizette would go through this amount of trouble to shame her. Lizette was so much better than that, or so Marnie had thought.

"Zee, I wish you would just —"

The sound of the homeroom bell reverberated throughout the hallway, interrupting Marnie and scattering a small group of curious students who were rubbernecking near Marnie's locker. Lizette rolled the dress up in a ball and tossed it into a wastebasket like a skilled point guard. Then she glowered at Marnie and said, "I'd rather get a new one."

As Lizette sashayed toward homeroom with Grier and Brynne at her side, Marnie was quite certain her so-called friend wasn't talking about just the dress.

Chapter 6

Nola couldn't concentrate on her book during Quiet Reading in English class. Nor could stop thinking about how she'd consoled Matt at his house yesterday. Although she hadn't stayed very long — Matt and his father had driven her back shortly after Mr. Heatherly had returned from Home Depot with what seemed like crates of supplies — Nola had felt like something special transpired between her and Matt. Nola had seen him at his most vulnerable and talked him through an overwhelming experience — in part because he chose to share his feelings with her instead of Riley.

However, every time she pictured the moment where she put her arms around Matt and hugged him, her brain flashed back to . . . her sweet, soft kiss with Ian! It was maddening — here Nola was on the brink of making headway with the guy she considered her soul mate, yet being haunted by the scent of Ian's musk cologne and the way he tasted like butterscotch. Shouldn't her brief bonding time with Matt have eradicated all memory of her smooch with the college boy? Or was her kiss with Ian too extraordinary and stupendous to forget?

Nola was pulled back into the real world when her teacher, Mr. Quinn, cleared his throat.

"All right, class. Now that you have examined the text for a while, I'd like those of you seated in the first and third rows to turn your desk around and have a discussion with the person behind you about the examples of imagery in this chapter," Mr. Quinn instructed. "And keep it *subdued,* please."

Nola groaned in dismay. She was in the third row, and seated behind her was none other than Weston Briggs.

"This'll be fun." His deep voice made Nola's eyelids twitch involuntarily.

"Oh, joy," Nola muttered as she picked up her desk and rotated it so she could face Weston.

The problem with facing Weston was this: Nola had to force herself not to be disarmed by his extremely fine Abercrombie-ness. It was an amazing feat, considering that today Weston had traded in his Red Sox hat and grass-stained baseball jersey for some well-applied hair wax and a blue V-neck Nautica sweater.

"So," Nola began with a lack of enthusiasm. "You have anything to say?"

Weston slid down in his seat and put his hands behind his head. "Not about imagery," he replied with a playful smile.

Nola rolled her eyes. "That was the assignment."

"But wouldn't you rather talk about other things, like . . . stuff we have in common?" Weston asked.

"You and I have *nothing* in common." Nola was two seconds away from turning her desk back around.

"Yeah, we do," Weston said, nodding to the right.

Nola peered over her shoulder and saw Marnie, slouched forward with her hand on her chin, staring out into space as Amanda Pfaffenbach, a notoriously chatty classmate, rambled on and on. It wasn't hard to notice how sad and listless Marnie appeared. The corners of her mouth were drooping low and the light pink tinge of her eyes was unmissable. Nola felt a pang of sympathy tweak her in the stomach.

"I'd rather not talk about me and Marnie," Nola said, turning to Weston. In fact, she'd rather not *think* about Marnie, either. Nola was just happy she'd fully recovered from her moment of weakness in front of Marnie's house and had pretty much put her ex-best friend out of her mind since then.

"Fine, let's talk about *me* and Marnie." Weston tapped Nola's foot with one of his Nike Air Diamonds. "Do you think she'll ever make out with me again?"

Nola laughed. "No. Way."

"How do you know? You two don't even hang

together anymore," Weston said, crossing his arms over his chest.

"Yeah, well, maybe you're right. She's not dating Dane anymore, so perhaps she'll make a trade," Nola said.

"And it's not like she has better options." Weston's smirk was positively disarming. "Now that Lizette and her friends have dumped her, too."

Nola's mouth grew slack. Lizette had kicked Marnie out of her inner circle? Talk about justice being served!

"When did this happen?"

Weston leaned forward and whispered, "At the secret password party."

"There was a secret password party?" Nola whispered back.

"Yeah, Majors only. Sorry," Weston said with a wink.

Ugh, what a freaking jerk!

"Whatever. Why did Marnie get the boot?"

"Apparently, Lizette found out that Miss Freshman Class Treasurer was sneaking around with her ex, Sawyer," Weston explained, keeping his voice low. "But Marnie denies it."

Nola felt as though she were an atom being split into two. On the one hand, she was absolutely thrilled that Marnie had been ousted by the shallow popular clique her former friend was so eager to be simpatico with. On the other hand, Nola knew that what had happened to Marnie was extremely unjust. Yes, Sawyer had been the object of Marnie's harmless obsession since grammar school and it was clear that Marnie was capable of being cruel and underhanded. Still, Nola was positive that Marnie didn't have it in her to outright cheat on Dane and betray Lizette all in one fell swoop. (At least, the Marnie who'd grown up with Nola didn't.)

The dismissal bell sent Weston off and running before he could finish his story, but Nola already got the picture. Dane had dumped Marnie because she had lost her exalted position in the Majors and her popularity stock had plummeted. And now Marnie dragged her heels sullenly and left the classroom without lifting her head up.

Once she was gone, Nola opened her bag and dug out Marnie's birthday bracelet. Nola knew if she gave this back to Marnie and told her that Dane and Lizette were most likely secret friends-with-benefits, Marnie would be crushed beyond recognition. Then again, Marnie might finally see Dane and Lizette for the lizards they were and beg Nola for forgiveness.

Either way, Nola would have to cross the battle lines in order to find out, but she wasn't ready to do that.

At least not yet.

* * *

Nola wasn't accustomed to showing up at her regular table in the cafeteria and finding only Evan Sanders there to greet her. She knew that Matt wasn't coming to school today — he and his father had to make another trip to Binghamton to meet with the detectives — but had no idea that Iris would be missing their usual chat 'n' chew. Now Nola would have to endure Evan's somewhat adoring/somewhat nervous glances and pray that he'd hide behind his trusty Sidekick instead of professing his not-so-secret crush.

Nola tottered over to her seat with her tray, which was filled to the edges with a fried fish sandwich, two dishes of pistachio pudding, and a side of macaroni and cheese. "Hey there."

Evan smoothed his hands over his supershort brown hair as Nola approached. Then for some strange reason, he tucked his white PROUD TO BE AWESOME T-shirt into his jeans and stood up when Nola set her tray on the table. Nola nodded and smiled, but Evan didn't sit down until after she did.

How . . . weird.

"Hi," Evan said, the corners of his mouth turning into a kind smile.

Although Nola felt extremely queasy, she couldn't help but smile back.

“Where’s Iris?” Nola hoped that from the squeakiness of her voice it wasn’t too obvious that she was uncomfortable being alone with him. Evan was such a nice guy, and for some reason, she felt like this question itself might hurt his feelings.

“She’s at the dentist, getting her braces put on.” Evan bowed his head and made the sign of the cross.

Nola giggled. “Wow, I don’t envy her.”

“I really like your teeth. They are so . . . *straight*,” Evan said awkwardly.

“Uh . . . thanks,” Nola replied, if not more awkwardly.

In an attempt to stall their conversation in its tracks, Nola shoveled as much pistachio pudding into her mouth that her straight teeth could handle. About five minutes went by without either of them saying a word. Evan typed on his Sidekick like a madman, looking up at Nola every so often as she gnawed on her fried fish sandwich. She thought that there was a chance he would be turned off if she slobbered all over herself like her little brothers, but at the same time, she had a little bit of pride, which she wasn’t too eager to give up.

“Nola,” Evan said when she took a break from her gorge-fest and sipped on her Canada Dry. “Can I ask you a question?”

Nola stopped mid-gulp. "Um, okay?" she said as her shins began to itch like crazy.

Evan put down his Sidekick and ran his hand through his hair. Then he coughed a little bit before saying, "What do you really think of the Magna Carta?"

Nola scratched at her leg and looked at Evan quizzically. Was this some sort of code for "Do you *like* me like me?" She certainly hoped not.

"I'm doing this opinion poll, for social studies class." Evan pulled out a pen and steno pad, rather official-like.

"Oh!" Nola said with relief. "That's . . . cool."

"Thanks," Evan said, his cheeks flushing a bit.

"Well, honestly, I think as far as English charters go, it's one of the best. After all, our Constitution was based on it," Nola commented.

Evan scribbled something down on his pad. "That's a very interesting point."

Nola didn't think so, but she had to admit, she kind of liked that Evan thought she was intelligent. In fact, her mood had definitely lightened. Maybe his crush on her had faded over the weekend and now he just saw her as a cotraveler on the road to academia.

"I have another question for you," Evan added, keeping his eyes fixed on his steno pad.

"What?"

"Would you go to the Homecoming dance with me?"

Nola sat there, completely dumbstruck. She had no clue how to respond, so she grabbed her Canada Dry can and chugged the rest of it. However, when she was through drinking her ginger ale, she answered Evan with a loud burp.

Oh, my god! That was repulsive!

"Was that . . . a yes?" Evan glanced up at her apprehensively as though he knew that was a huge reach.

Nola grinned at him. Not too many guys would be sweet enough to turn a belch into a gracious acceptance of a Homecoming dance invitation. Still Nola wasn't sure if she wanted to say yes. Sure, Evan was nice, and smart, and . . . nice. But she didn't have that magnetic attraction to him like she did with Matt, or the antagonistic-yet-titillating vibe she felt with Ian. Did she really want to be his date to the dance, knowing that he had feelings for her that she didn't return?

Then again, would she get asked by anyone else? Matt would probably dress up in a suit and bring gorgeous Riley Finnegan to the dance, where they'd cling to each other while swaying to a slow song. If Nola didn't say yes to Evan, she'd just sit at home and wonder if she could have stolen one moment with Matt for herself. And if Nola did say yes, she'd be able to show Marnie just how good she was doing on her own.

Still, Nola felt a little bad that she was about to accept Evan's invitation for reasons that didn't involve him at all.

"All right, Evan. I'll go," Nola said, her grin weak and unsteady.

But Evan didn't seem to notice. He was too busy saying "Thank you" over and over.

Chapter 7

Marnie didn't even bother going to the cafeteria during her lunch period. Not only was she convinced she would never have an appetite again, but she was also certain that she wouldn't be able to stand being cast as the lead character in the horror flick *The Scourge of Lizette Levin: Cross Me and Die a Gruesome Death, Part 2.* The only recourse Marnie had was to sneak into the school auditorium and curl up in one of the back-row seats.

She'd been staring at the words to Poughkeepsie Central's alma mater for fifteen minutes, hoping that she'd discover some nugget of wisdom that would help her dig herself out of the twelve-foot grave she'd been buried alive in. However, there wasn't much she could take away from a song with lines like "Bequeath thy gallant spirit, mighty hawks" and "Hither to the clouds on wings of adulation." As Marnie brought up her legs to her chest and rested her chin on her knees, she wasn't sure if there was anything that could comfort her at a time like this.

And then something unexpected happened. Marnie smiled at a warm, familiar memory of an event that had taken place a few years ago in an auditorium not unlike this one. Back in fourth grade, Marnie had talked Nola into signing up for their grammar school talent show. Or perhaps a bribe had been involved. Marnie couldn't quite remember. But she did recall the day of the show vividly.

Marnie and Nola had been practicing their act for weeks — Marnie choreographed a dance/jump-rope routine while Nola picked the song: "Can't Get You Out of My Head" by Kylie Minogue. The morning of the contest, Marnie and Nola had looked sassy in their matching silver-sequined shorts and black bodysuits (which Mrs. Fitzpatrick bought at a discount Danskin store). Only there'd been one little snafu. Nola had been so nervous that she'd broken out in hives — on her *face*. Dark red splotches covered her cheeks and forehead and nose. Still, when the curtain had come up and their act was announced, Nola didn't miss a beat. She went through the whole routine, scratching at her skin whenever she could, just because she'd known how much the show had meant to Marnie.

Suddenly, another line from the alma mater seemed to resonate more: "Standing hand in hand, loyal until the end."

"Mind if I join you?"

Marnie lifted her head and looked to her right.

Standing in the aisle was none other than Sawyer Lee, hands in his pockets, dark eyes as iridescent as a gemstone.

"Sorry, just thought you might like some company," he said nonchalantly.

Marnie put her feet down on the floor and pulled on the hem of her skirt anxiously. Obviously, Sawyer had heard about what had gone down at the most awful inauguration party in American history. "Um . . . yeah, I do. Thanks."

Sawyer sat down next to Marnie, but kept his gaze on the stage in front of them. It was a while before he said anything, but Marnie didn't really notice. She was too preoccupied with studying her favorite of Sawyer's features — his taut, smooth skin; his long, full eyelashes; his slightly pug nose. Being this close to him was almost intoxicating.

"So, how does it feel?" Sawyer asked, his cheeks reddening quickly, like he'd just gotten sunburn. "You know, to be humiliated in front of people for no reason at all?"

The pseudo-intoxicated sensation had just left Marnie's body like an exorcized ghost. She was completely remorseful about ragging Sawyer in order to please Lizette, but now that he was calling Marnie on her BS, she was especially ashamed of herself.

"Sawyer, I'm *so* sorry for what I said," Marnie murmured. "I was just . . . in a tough spot. I didn't know what to do."

Sawyer sighed heavily. "Yes, you did. You just cared more about making Lizette mad than you did about hurting me."

Marnie bristled at Sawyer's chiding. Did he have any idea how difficult that situation had been for her? Or how horrible she'd felt afterward? "It's not that simple. Lizette is my friend. I had to stick by her."

"Right," he replied, rolling his eyes incredulously.

"God, why doesn't anyone believe *anything* I say?" Marnie's voice raised an octave with each word. "I mean it, Sawyer. I'm really sorry. *Really.*"

Sawyer smiled against his will and glanced at Marnie. "*Really* sorry, huh?"

"Really," Marnie said, wiping a stray tear from her eye and kind of giggling at the same time. "Really, *really.*"

"Then I guess we're cool." Sawyer reached over and took Marnie's hand, lightly rubbing her palm with his thumb.

At first, all Marnie could think of was how unbelievably soft Sawyer's skin was and how every part of her body was tingling (even her appendix, which was considered to be pretty much useless by most scientists).

But then Erin's voice began echoing in the recesses of her mind, telling her that holding Sawyer's hand was very much the opposite of avoiding him like a homeless man.

Marnie knew that Erin couldn't have been more accurate in her assessment. If Marnie wanted back in with Lizette and the Majors — and she did, regardless of how badly Lizette was behaving — she couldn't get close to Sawyer.

This was a sacrifice that had to be made.

Slowly, Marnie pulled her hand out of Sawyer's grasp and looked down at her lap. "I — I can't do this."

"Can't do what?" Sawyer sounded disappointed already.

"Hang out with you," Marnie croaked.

Argh! What am I saying?!?!

"Why not?"

"Like I told you before. Because of Lizette."

This time, Sawyer's sigh seemed to last for hours. "Marnie, I *like* you. *A lot.*"

A molten-lava-type heat shot up Marnie's spine. Sawyer Lee just admitted to *liking* her! A LOT!

"But maybe you're right. We shouldn't hang out." Sawyer stood up. "At least not until you realize who your true friends are."

Marnie was kind of surprised when Sawyer agreed to cool things off so quickly. But when he walked out of the auditorium without saying another word, she realized that one of her true friends had just slipped through the back door.

Marnie nearly cursed out loud during study hall when she heard a voice roar over the intercom in the library:

"Marnie Fitzpatrick, please report to the guidance office. Marnie Fitzpatrick, to the guidance office. Thank you!"

After picking up her notebook and slinging her bag over her shoulder, Marnie trudged out of the room and down the hallway as though she were on death row. Marnie knew that guidance counselor extraordinaire Mrs. Robertson wanted a progress report on Marnie and Weston Briggs, the most ridiculous pairing in Poughkeepsie Central's Best Buddy program. Except there wasn't a lot to report — although Weston had comforted Marnie on Saturday night after the smackdown to end all smackdowns, her intensely negative feelings about her ex-boyfriend hadn't progressed very much.

As Marnie approached the guidance office, she decided that she was going to bow out of the program. While she was running the risk of disappointing Mrs. Robertson and having one less extracurricular to put on her college apps, Marnie was stressed enough as it was without having to worry about walking Weston around school like a show pony.

Mrs. Robertson was waiting for Marnie at the door with a pleasant smile on her face and a purple hand-knit shawl around her shoulders. "Hi, Marnie."

"Hi, Mrs. Robertson," she replied halfheartedly.

Mrs. Robertson gestured to her room. "Your buddy is already here, so go on in. I'll be with you both in a minute."

Yeah, right. My buddy.

Marnie slogged ahead with her head tilted down, indicating just how little she was looking forward to this meeting. But Mrs. Robertson flitted off, leaving Marnie to slug it out with Mr. Baseball Fever all by herself.

"I don't think Mrs. Ro liked what I had to say, Marnie."

Mrs. Robertson's desk chair spun around slowly and there sat Weston, adorned with a dubious yet sexy grin that Marnie used to love.

"Is this the face of a person who cares?" Marnie said, scowling.

Weston's eyes sparkled as he leaped up and ambled over to her. "Actually, that's the face of a person who owes me."

Marnie flinched. "What? I don't owe you a damn thing."

"Just wait," Weston said in a haughty tone.

All of a sudden, Mrs. Robertson walked in with a huge binder. "Okay, I'm ready to sit down and talk business. How about you?"

Marnie gazed at her guidance counselor confusedly and took a seat next to Weston. "I guess so."

"Great," Mrs. Robertson said. "Marnie, Weston has already brought me up to speed. I'm sorry that the in-school buddy system isn't working out for you two."

Marnie flinched again. Weston had told Mrs. Robertson that they weren't Best Buddy material? Wasn't that supposed to be *her* line? Marnie had to admit it stung a little to know that Weston didn't want to be around her, even though she could barely put up with him.

"That's okay," Weston said with a playful smile. "I think that getting more involved with student government will help me raise my profile. It worked for you, didn't it, Marnie?"

"Yeah, I suppose." Marnie huffed and crossed her arms over her chest.

"And once baseball season takes off in the spring, I'll be golden," Weston proclaimed.

"I'm sure you will," Mrs. Robertson said, shaking her head as though she'd heard it all. "Okay then, consider your Best Buddy relationship dissolved."

It was bizarre. Marnie had come into the guidance office *wanting* this to happen, but now that it had, she felt very lonely. Sure, Weston was far from being her friend, but at least with him as her Best Buddy she would have had someone to hang out with, even if she was duty-bound.

"You're free to go," Mrs. Robertson said as she opened her binder and began to whip through the pages.

As Weston nabbed his book bag and started rifling through it in his chair, Marnie came to another realization. Erin had told Marnie earlier that she needed to start chilling with another guy so that Lizette and everyone else at school could see that Marnie wasn't into Sawyer. Since she had already dated Weston and had nothing but disdain for him, wouldn't he be the perfect boy to have a fake fling with? This way, Marnie could drop him once she was back in the Majors, without having any regrets.

"Wait!" Marnie yelped out of the blue.

Weston and Mrs. Robertson both looked at her strangely.

"What's wrong?" Mrs. Robertson asked.

Marnie deeply inhaled. "Um . . . I think Weston and I should give the Best Buddy program another try."

For the second time today, Marnie was hearing herself say the most insane things.

"Really?" Mrs. Robertson sounded skeptical. "Weston, how do you feel about it?"

Marnie looked at Weston, who seemed pretty baffled. "Uh . . . I don't know. I wasn't expecting this."

Neither was I.

"Well, there aren't many days left in October," Marnie reasoned. "I'd hate to quit now."

"I see." Mrs. Robertson scratched her chin with a pencil. "I'm fine with reinstating you both, but Marnie, you're going to have to spend a lot more time with Weston. I hear you were shirking your responsibilities."

Marnie narrowed her eyes at Weston. *What. A. PEON!*

"Do you agree to those terms?" Mrs. Robertson asked her.

"Yes, I do," Marnie said, a bit unconvincingly.

Mrs. Robertson pointed at Weston with her pencil. "What about you?"

"Um . . . uh . . . yeah, sure," Weston stammered.

"Good. Let's meet again after Homecoming, okay?" Mrs. Robertson said cheerily. "Now get going. I have tons of work to catch up on."

Marnie waved good-bye and scurried out of the office before a stupefied Weston could ask her why she'd gone totally mental. But a quick exit didn't stop Marnie from asking herself the same question all day.

Chapter 8

When Nola came home from school late Monday afternoon, it took her a moment to absorb the scene in front of her. Not only were Dennis and Dylan climbing over every piece of furniture and screaming at sonic-blast levels, but it looked as though strip miners had been hard at work in the James home. A vase that had been filled with fresh sunflowers early this morning was now on the floor, the petals scattered all over the carpet. Several framed photographs that had been neatly arranged on top of the cherry-wood hutch were practically demolished. Food was even sticking to the windows!

Nola was completely aghast. The boys had only been home for twenty minutes and Ian was supposed to be watching them.

As soon as his name registered in her brain, Nola shivered. She'd been imagining their kiss on and off for days, but she hadn't really considered what would happen when she faced Ian again. She figured that he might act a bit aloof toward her, or fumble through an apology of some sort. However, Nola realized that as she wasted time speculating on what Ian might do, her brothers had just knocked into her mother's favorite figurine.

Immediately, Nola dropped her book bag and leaped forward like a superhero, catching it in her hands before it crashed to the ground.

Dennis and Dylan came to a screeching halt when they saw the irritated expression on Nola's face as she looked up at them from the living room floor.

"Where. Is. Ian?" she asked, clenching her jaw so tightly she feared it might snap at the hinges.

"In the kitchen," Dylan replied, right before getting crushed by a pile-driving Dennis.

"Take that, traitor!" Dennis yelled at the top of his lungs.

"Quit it, guys." Nola got up and gripped the figurine in her hands protectively. "I mean it, or you'll be in deep trouble."

"Ooooooh, scary!" Dennis jeered.

Dylan nailed Dennis in the shins with the sole of his high-top sneakers, which sent the scoundrels running out of the room and in opposite directions.

Nola rolled her eyes and trudged into the kitchen, steadying herself for her first post-kiss Ian confrontation.

Ian was reclining back in a chair, his feet propped up on the table, eyes on the pages of a red paperback book. Of course, Ian looked remarkably hot, even in one of his uptight argyle sweater vests. But what really stood out — other than his glossy brown hair and the cute way he was pursing his lips — were the silver wire-rimmed glasses that had slid down to the end of his nose. They made him look unbelievably . . . irresistible. In fact, Nola was so enraptured with the sight of him that she nearly let the sculpture slip through her fingers.

However, when a loud crashing sound came from the ceiling above them, Nola was so startled that she ended up dropping it on one of her size eight-and-a-half feet.

"Yeeeeooow!" Nola yelped, clutching the part of her foot where her big toe used to be.

As for Ian, he barely lifted his smoldering eyes from his book. "Careful," he muttered, turning a page so briskly that he could have given himself a paper cut.

Nola was too busy wincing in pain to notice how pompous Ian had just sounded. She breathed a sigh of relief, though, when she saw that the sculpture hadn't broken. Apparently, her more-than-ample-size foot was enough to cushion its fall.

Nola limped over to the table and sat in a chair next to Ian. As she massaged the feeling back into her toes, she kept her gaze trained on his forehead like she was trying to read his thoughts. Ironically, she couldn't really keep track of her own right now. Visions of Ian leaning in and pressing his tender, butterscotch-infused lips against hers were blurring with images of Matt wrapping his arms around her as though he was holding on for dear life.

All of a sudden, Ian closed his book and put it down on the table. Then he crossed his arms over his chest gruffly. "Do you mind? I'm trying to study."

His curt tone yanked Nola's head out of the clouds.

Well, that wasn't quite romantic, was it?

"Aren't you supposed to be watching Dennis and Dylan? It's like Doomsday in the living room."

"I've got it under control. So don't worry about it," Ian said sharply.

Nola inhaled and exhaled, so she could retain her cool. She didn't want to jump to any conclusions. After all, Ian had been very sweet to her last week, letting down his guard and showing Nola that he had a warm and kind side to him. Not only that but he'd also said she was beautiful and went so far as to show her that he believed it by bestowing Nola with the most delicious first kiss ever. She owed him the benefit of the doubt, right? Maybe he was just having a bad day.

"Well, while they were going nuts in there, they almost broke my mom's figurine." Nola stretched over to where it was lying on the kitchen floor tiles, picked it up, and put it in her lap. "I think that magic hand-clap of yours is kind of overdue."

"Are you saying that I'm slacking off, or that I don't know how to do my job?" Ian asked snidely.

Okay, I can't believe I let this guy's mouth anywhere near me.

"I'm not saying either of those things," Nola said, the tempo of her pulse increasing. "I just —"

"Spare me the excuses." Ian pushed back from the table, his cheeks blazing red, and shot up. "I know when I'm being second-guessed."

"No one is second-guessing you, Ian."

"Really? Because usually when someone interferes, it means that they don't trust you."

Nola set her mother's sculpture firmly on the kitchen table and rose to her feet, one of which was still throbbing mercilessly. "I'm *not* interfering!"

"Yes, you are."

"Actually, I was trying to *help* you."

"How is pointing out the obvious helping me?" Ian barked, taking a few steps toward Nola.

"I don't know. How is reading a book in the kitchen considered babysitting my little brothers?" Nola snapped back.

"I *said* I was *studying*!"

Nola was so flustered that all she could say in response was, "Whoop-dee-freaking-doo!"

Rather than breaking the tension in the room like most lame comebacks do, Nola's flippant comment seemed to anger Ian to the point where she thought he might blow a gasket. But instead of finishing her off with a brutal remark, Ian looked up to the ceiling and sighed, as though he was giving up on something.

He kept his gaze there for a while, both of them listening to Dennis and Dylan scrambling down the upstairs hallway and shrieking. Then Ian set his eyes back on Nola, who couldn't help but notice the weary and strained expression on his gorgeous face. He reached out and ran his hand down the length of her arm, gently taking her hand in his and locking fingers with her.

When Nola felt him squeeze her hand, her body went limp. Was Ian about to kiss her again? She hoped that he would, and at the same time, she didn't. During crises like these, Nola wished that she could freeze-frame the moment and call Marnie for her boy expertise.

But Nola was safe for now. Ian let go of her hand and left the kitchen. As she heard Ian climb the stairs, she picked up the book he was reading and looked at the cover.

Lolita.

Monday, October 15, 8:03 P.M.

flowerpower: *owie ow ow*

nolaj1994: ☹ *ur mouth hurts, huh?*

flowerpower: *of course, i just had metal soldered to my teeth*

nolaj1994: *sorry. anything I can do?*

flowerpower: *distract me*

nolaj1994: *how?*

flowerpower: *tell me a story*

nolaj1994: *about what?*

flowerpower: *hmmm . . . let's c . . . u & sanders going 2 the homecoming dance together?*

nolaj1994: *oh brother*

flowerpower: *don't hold out on me, nol. i'm handicapped*

nolaj1994: *not really, u can still annoy me without talking*

flowerpower: *touché! now tell me what happened*

nolaj1994: *there's not much 2 say, he asked and i said yes*

flowerpower: *i said distract me, not bore me*

nolaj1994: *what do u want me 2 do? make something up?*

flowerpower: *have a feeling that would b boring 2*

nolaj1994: *sigh*

flowerpower: *ian will b heartbroken 2 hear about ur new bf*

nolaj1994: *evan is NOT my bf, and ian wouldn't care anyway*

flowerpower: *yeah right! ian wants u 2 b his sex kitten*

nolaj1994: *omg, r u for real?*

flowerpower: *u bettah believe it!*

nolaj1994: *well i should go, homework & stuff*

flowerpower: *fine, abandon me*

nolaj1994: *i'm not abandoning u!*

flowerpower: *yes u r, it's ok*

nolaj1994: *just 1 quick thing b4 i go*

flowerpower: *shoot*

nolaj1994: *do u believe it's possible 2 4give & 4get?*

flowerpower: *yeah, i think so, but it depends on how badly a person has been hurt*

nolaj1994: *ur right.*

flowerpower: *of course i am*

nolaj1994: ☺

flowerpower: *now go do ur homework*

nolaj1994: *thanks, iris*

flowerpower: *c ya*

nolaj1994: *bye!*

Chapter 9

When Marnie woke up early Tuesday morning, she tried to convince herself that by the law of averages, today would be infinitely better than yesterday. As she got ready for school, she primped as though she hadn't cried before she went to sleep last night. She layered on her favorite shades of M.A.C. makeup and smoothed out her wavy blonde locks with her sister's professional-strength ionic flat iron (which Erin had forgotten to unplug from the outlet in the bathroom, of course). Then she pulled on a pair of her favorite wide-leg jeans and a magenta puff-sleeve, smocked-bodice top, both secretly purchased online at Mandee.

At around 7:30 A.M., Marnie went to the kitchen, opened the freezer, and snatched a box of blueberry Toaster Strudel, which teetered on top of a large stack of microwavable meals. When one flaky strudel was in the toaster, her mother came up behind her, all fresh-faced, power-suited, and ready to show homes to eager real-estate buyers. Everything seemed so normal and routine that Marnie had actually forgotten that she'd blown off Sawyer Lee in order to salvage her relationship with certain mega Majors.

Until her mother said something earth-shattering while making a pot of hazelnut coffee.

"So Erin tells me that you're the talk of the school these days."

Marnie squeezed the vanilla icing packet so hard that some of it sprayed onto the countertop near the sink. Erin had spent most of Sunday on her cell and was currently passed out in her bedroom because she'd been out partying with her former Homecoming court all of yesterday. How could Erin have possibly had time to rat her out to her mom? Obviously her sister found Marnie's excommunication from the PoCen in-crowd so heinously embarrassing that it warranted an emergency meeting with their mother.

So much for sisterly love.

"Really? What else did Erin tell you?" Marnie's blood was boiling like potent chemicals in a science lab beaker.

"That Lizette and Dane fed you to the wolves," Mrs. Fitzpatrick replied as she gave her daughter a pitying look. "Are you okay?"

"I'm fine, Mom." Marnie went back to icing her strudel and prayed that the conversation would end there.

Apparently, whoever was in charge of prayer-answering this morning was busy doing something else.

"Well, Erin told me that she gave you some great tips on how to handle the situation." Marnie's mom poured some half-and-half into her coffee mug and stirred it with a spoon. "So I wouldn't worry. You'll be back in with Lizette and Dane in no time at all."

Marnie rolled her eyes. If she had to listen to more of her mother's pro-Erin propaganda, she just might swallow some cyanide. However, Marnie was not able to get her hands on any of the poison and therefore had to listen to her mother prattle on and on about Erin's vast knowledge on all things popularity-related and how Marnie should be thanking the masters of providence for blessing her with a sister like Erin. Arriving at Poughkeepsie Central to face the whispers, snickers, and cold shoulders suddenly seemed like a Key West vacation.

But when Marnie got out of the Corolla and set foot on school grounds, she realized how far she was from a tropical getaway. In fact, this morning the cold shoulders were tundralike. The news of Marnie's falling out with Lizette and her breakup with Dane had obviously hit the ears of everyone in the freshman class, if not the entire school. No one was even looking in her direction when she walked by. It was as though she were living in a Hans Christian Andersen fairy tale and a wart-covered witch had put some sort of transparency spell on her.

Even Marnie's teachers seemed to be ignoring her. During English class, Mr. Quinn forgot to call her name during roll and when he handed back some graded quiz papers, everyone else received their work except for Marnie. Mr. Quinn said he didn't remember what had happened to her quiz, but at this point, Marnie was convinced that Brynne the gap-toothed demon had managed to turn Mr. Quinn against her, too.

By the time class was over, Marnie was near tears. The pressure and tension she felt weighing on her heart were unbearable. Actually, breathing in and out had suddenly become excruciatingly painful. Marnie was concerned she might be going berserk, so she attempted to inhale deeply, just as the ultraflexible instructor at Arlington YogaWorks had taught her.

Thankfully, the bell rang, and Marnie sighed in relief. She was free next period and would definitely be spending it with Nurse Mulchahy. At least there, she'd be with someone who cared for her. True, it was Nurse Mulchahy's *job* to care for people, but Marnie wasn't going to get bogged down with semantics at a critical moment like this.

Marnie eagerly collected her textbook and put it in her tote bag while Weston Briggs shuffled by her and lightly pinched her on the waist.

"Jerk," Marnie mumbled as Weston left the room, grinning like he'd just hit a double in a close-scoring baseball game. The fact that she had arranged to be "buddies" with Weston was just further evidence of how desperate she was for an ally.

"Hey," a voice murmured from off to the left.

Marnie turned and saw Nola James standing a few feet away with one hand in her pocket and the other clenched into a fist.

Even though Nola looked as though she was ready to sock someone in the gut, Marnie was actually a little happy to see her. Marnie really didn't want to live in a world where the only person who spoke to her was Weston Briggs. But when Erin's advice about friends and enemies rattled around Marnie's brain, she hardened her heart and glowered at Nola.

"What do *you* want?" Marnie stiffened her shoulders.

Nola bristled when she heard the pointed tone of Marnie's voice. "I found something that belongs to you."

"I don't remember losing anything," Marnie replied.

Nola's rigid stance loosened and she broke into a fit of laughter.

"Did I say something *funny?*" Marnie asked, angrily thrusting her hands on her hips.

"More like ironic," Nola said, smirking.

"What*ever,*" Marnie huffed.

Nola raised her arm and held out her hand. Marnie couldn't believe her own eyes. In Nola's palm was the bracelet that she had made for Marnie's birthday. Marnie was frozen in shock. How had Nola gotten it back from the clutches of Lizette Levin? She almost didn't want to know.

Nola frowned once she realized Marnie wasn't going to move or make a sound. "Never mind. It was stupid of me to think that you'd want it back," she snapped.

Marnie felt like her head was a balloon. She had no clue what to think or say. "Where did you get that?"

"It was on the floor of Dane's car," Nola said.

Now Marnie felt like someone had stuck a ten-foot needle in her balloonlike head.

Nola *was in* Dane's *car?!*!

"What the hell were *you* doing in Dane's Jag, you little twerp?" Marnie demanded, practically spitting nails.

Nola let out a sarcastic laugh. "Oh, my god. Do you think I'd stoop so *low* as to get with Dane 'Slimeball' Harris? Please!"

Marnie's stomach churned. Nola was getting way too good at this smack-talk thing.

"Yeah, right! Like Dane would even think twice about *you,*" Marnie barked. It dawned on her that she was defending the guy who had dumped her the moment he thought his reputation was at stake. Still, it was up to Marnie to put Nola in her place.

"Here's a news flash for you. I can get *any* guy I want," Nola said with a cocky smile. "And I wouldn't want Dane in *a million years*. Neither should you, if you ask me."

Marnie sneered at Nola, even though she knew deep down her ex-friend was probably right. Dane had conned Marnie into thinking he was genuinely hot for her and then snuffed her out like she didn't even matter. That was certainly enough to get him elected to the Slimeball Hall of Fame.

Nola carelessly tossed the bracelet onto the desk in front of Marnie as though it was a piece of trash. "Instead of jumping to conclusions about me and Dane" — Nola stuck her finger in her mouth and pretended to gag — "why don't you ask yourself what Dane and *Lizette* are up to? I'm sure this bracelet didn't fall off her wrist on its own. Catch my drift?"

And with that, Nola spun on her heel and briskly strode out the door.

Marnie thought about running after Nola and asking her if she knew for a fact that something dicey had gone on between Dane and Lizette, but instead Marnie threw the bracelet into her bag and yanked the zipper so hard that she nearly ripped it from the seams. Marnie had suspected before that Dane and Lizette were secretly hooking up, but she didn't want to find out from Nola. Marnie wanted to uncover the truth herself.

At first, she wasn't quite sure how she was going to gather her evidence. However, when Marnie stormed out of the room and spotted Dane and Lizette in the hallway, laughing flirtatiously, an inspired idea came to her — courtesy of a gap-toothed demon.

Chapter 10

"This is *disgusting*!" Iris bellowed after she sipped a banana-flavored protein shake through a straw. "I should sue the president of the company for false advertising. See, right here on the label it says it tastes delicious!"

Nola mindlessly poked at her Wednesday lunch special (mystery meat and crinkle fries) with her fork, only half-listening to Iris's whining. Nola had been in a fog since yesterday morning's sparring match with Marnie and was still kicking herself every ten minutes for approaching her ex-friend with the bracelet. How could she have thought she'd be able to forgive and forget with Marnie? Probably because Nola had managed to convince herself that Marnie was going to be touched by her gesture and feel indebted to Nola for trying to set her straight about her so-called friends.

But what was clouding Nola's mind even more was something that she'd said to Marnie in the heat of battle.

I can get any guy I want.

Nola was sure that Marnie had thought her gloating was based on pure fiction, but the truth was, Nola had been a boy magnet lately. Evan had asked her to the

Homecoming dance. Ian — who was a *college guy*, thank you very much — couldn't keep his lips to himself the other night. Even she and Matt seemed to be growing closer to each other these days. Nola had to admit, having all these male admirers felt pretty damn good.

However, not so good that she could overlook the fact that she didn't have the one guy she truly wanted.

"How many times do I have to tell you that crash dieting isn't the answer, Iris?"

Matt sauntered over to their regular table in the cafeteria, brown paper lunch bag in his hand and unkempt hair falling in his eyes. Right behind him was an extremely well-groomed Evan, who was wearing a striped button-down shirt and a pair of black pants instead of his usual Whacker attire.

When the boys sat down across from Iris, Nola had no trouble interpreting the sly expression on Matt's face. Evan was obviously trying to impress Nola with his dapper look. And it was working. With his bashful smile and wide-eyed innocence, Evan appeared as though he should be on the cover of *J-14* as a new Disney Channel heartthrob.

Nola gulped and crossed her legs.

"I'm not crash dieting, nimrod," Iris said to Matt, kicking him under the table. "It still hurts to chew."

"Oh, right! I can't believe I almost forgot about the braces." Matt reached into his bag, pulled out a large orange, and started to peel it.

"Of course you forgot." Iris pushed her shake aside and massaged her jaw. "You were too busy giving Sanders here a *Queer Eye* makeover."

Nola had never wanted to swat Iris more. Why did she always have to say such brazen things? Especially when she knew how uncomfortable it made Nola.

Oddly enough, though, Evan didn't seem affected by Iris's remark. In fact, he just grinned at Nola like she was the only person at the table and said, "I won the Baltus Van Kleeck Scholarship. That's why I'm dressed like this. I have to go to a recipient banquet right after school."

Nola brightened a little on hearing this news, but surprisingly, she felt a tad let down that his snappy get-up wasn't because of her. "You did? That's great."

Matt slapped Evan on the back and smiled in appreciation. "Sure is. Our boy here is on his way to becoming a National Merit freak, I can feel it."

Evan chuckled. "I wouldn't get your hopes up."

"Well, congrats on being such an egghead, Ev," Iris said, her lackluster tone indicating that she wasn't the slightest bit interested in this conversation. "I'm going to get some chocolate pudding. Maybe that'll take the edge off."

"Just watch the calories. You want to fit into your Homecoming dress, don't you?" Matt teased.

"News flash, Lint-for-brains. I'm not going to Homecoming. I forgot I have debate camp next weekend," Iris snipped.

"Debate camp, huh? Well, that's . . . swell," Matt said, laughing.

Iris mouthed an obscene set of words to Matt as she rose from her seat and then stormed off to the chilled-foods section of the cafeteria.

Immediately, Nola's toes began to itch. She was now alone with Matt and Evan, which always made her feel a bit jumpy. However, that was before she knew that Evan had a crush on her and that Matt had been aware of this from the first day they'd met.

"Soooooo," Matt said not-so-innocuously. "What's new with you two?"

Nola knocked Matt in the leg with her foot.

"Ow! Why is everyone kicking me today?"

"Because you are being *stupid*," Nola said, gnashing her teeth.

"Oh, I didn't know those were the rules," Evan quipped before stomping on Matt's Converse with his Rockport loafers.

“C’mon, man! I have to dance on these in a week.” Matt winced.

“Yeah, well, Nola and I will make sure to take cover,” Evan said, winking at her.

Nola had to admit, Evan seemed different today. Instead of taking refuge behind one of his gadgets, he was really coming out of his shell and showing his light-hearted and humorous side. Nola found it quite appealing, and for the first time, she could see why Matt and Evan were close friends.

Matt gestured to the clock on the wall. “Dude, aren’t you supposed to be meeting with Principal Baxter about the banquet?”

Evan’s eyes widened to the size of half-dollars. “Crap, I’m late.”

“I’d run if I were you,” Matt said.

Evan hopped up and began to sprint away. But once he reached the cafeteria door, he turned around and came back to say something to Nola.

“I’ll call you later about the dance, okay?”

“Okay,” she mumbled.

Evan put a hand on her shoulder and squeezed it affectionately. “See ya.”

Then he was gone.

Matt leaned over the table and patted Nola on the head like a puppy. “Aaawwww, somebody’s smitten!”

Instead of responding, Nola just rolled her eyes.

The irony just keeps on coming.

"I've never seen a guy so excited about a dance before." Matt popped a wedge of orange in his mouth. "With the exception of Kevin Bacon in *Footloose,* that is."

Nola put her elbows on the table and covered her face with her hands.

"What's the matter, Nol?"

Nola could tell by the nuances of Matt's voice that he wasn't playing around with her anymore. He was sincerely concerned.

"I'm just . . . worried," she muttered.

"About what?"

Nola moved her hands from her face to the back of her neck, which she began to rub. "About the dance. About Evan. About Evan and me at the dance — *together*."

"Uh-huh." Matt smiled, taking a slice of orange and offering it to Nola. "Have some. Vitamin C kills everything, especially worry."

Nola's heart always got warm when Matt made her laugh. "Thanks," she said, and took the orange slice. When she ate it, the sweetness of the juice lingered on her tongue.

"Listen, I know you're anxious, but you're going to have a lot of fun. And ever since you said yes to Evan, he's been, like, bouncing off the walls," Matt said. "Just relax and enjoy all the attention he's going to lavish on you."

Nola's heart went from warm to frigid in a matter of milliseconds. "What do you mean by that?"

"I can't say. It's a secret between dudes." Matt bit into another orange slice and grinned impishly. However, once Nola kicked Matt in the leg, he spit it out.

"Was I being stupid again?"

"Yes. Very."

Matt sighed. "Okay, fine. He's planning on taking you to a romantic and expensive dinner before the dance. And then afterward, I think he's going to set up some sort of laser-light show."

All of a sudden, the blood in Nola's head rushed down to her feet.

"Nola, what's the matter? You're looking really pale."

"It sounds like . . . a date."

"Oh, it's a date, all right. Pretty standard fare, though, minus the laser show. But so what? You've been on dates before, haven't you?"

Nola shook her head so hard that her ponytail nearly smacked her in the nose.

"Wow. That's . . . wow."

"Great, now you think I'm a loser."

"Nola, I would never think you're a loser. Actually, I think all the guys in this dinky town are. How could no one have asked you out?"

Nola broke into a shy smile.

"Wait a second, I've got an idea," Matt said while snapping his fingers.

Oh no.

"You need a warm-up date, or a dry run, so you won't be as nervous about Homecoming." Matt scooted over so that he was sitting right next to Nola. "Picture it. Me and you. Saturday night. Dinner and a movie. Or something less cliché. Either way, you can practice all of your smooth moves on me." Matt put his arm around Nola and brought her in for a brief hug. "What do you think?"

Nola knew that what she was thinking was a far cry from what she was going to say. This idea was preposterous! And what kind of idiot would agree to a *fake* date with the boy she had a crush on, just so that she could be less anxious on a *real* date with the boy who had a crush on *her*?

Apparently, an idiot who was both madly in love and a masochist.

"I think I should get to pick the movie," Nola said while gazing into Matt's shining eyes.

"Sounds more than fair." Matt tugged on Nola's ponytail playfully like she was his kid sister. "Besides, I always let Riley pick the flick when we go out. It's the gentlemanly thing to do."

Chapter 11

HOW TO CATCH LIZETTE AND DANE RED-HANDED, AN ANNOTATED LIST

1) Develop stealthy Bond girl tendencies! Must be able to crouch down low and lurk around dark corners, which means mastering those yoga poses.
2) Wear camouflage-type colors. Earth tones will help me blend in!
3) Borrow Mom's opera glasses for long-range vision (sort of).
4) Stick close to my target, but stay far enough away so I won't get caught (just like Brynne's spy has).

Thursday afternoon's student council meeting was just another painful reminder of how miserable Marnie's high school existence was going to be without Lizette Levin. Marnie hadn't been addressing the crowd for more than a minute about Saturday's freshman class car wash fund-raiser when she looked up from her flash cards and noticed that everyone was talking over her. It was like she was Miss Peters, the most notoriously boring teacher at Poughkeepsie Central. Marnie nervously tugged at the collar of her black semi-sheer batiste top as perspiration trickled down the back of her neck.

Maybe the podium microphone isn't working.

Marnie inspected the audio equipment for frayed wires and such, but there didn't seem to be any technical glitch. The thing that was preventing Marnie's fellow classmates from acknowledging her authority as freshman class treasurer was a horrible excuse for a person, who had cornered herself off in the back row of lecture hall four, where she was pointing and laughing at Marnie constantly.

The horrible person was Brynne, of course, and although she didn't have Lizette as her cohort today, she had recruited several other high-powered Majors into her tangled web of viciousness. Even the Leeks, who had really admired Marnie for her hard-fought campaign and landslide of a win, were too busy whispering to one another and snickering to pay attention to Marnie's speech.

Marnie ordered her shaking legs to stand firm and her lower lip to stop trembling, but no matter how much she wanted to show Brynne that she couldn't be pushed around, she wasn't able to withstand the torture any longer. Without getting to the end of her flash cards for the second time in less than a week, Marnie shuffled back to her seat in the center of the empty front row, completely defeated and dejected.

Just then Marnie felt her Razr buzzing in her denim skirt pocket. She scooped it out and warily checked her messages. There were three texts, all from a number that she didn't recognize, each one of them meaner than the one before.

U SUCK!!!
QUIT NOW, LOSER
BETTER WATCH UR BACK

It was enough to send Marnie into a full retreat. She grabbed the rest of her belongings and sprinted out the door.

Marnie did her best to maintain her composure and keep her satin lace-up boot-clad feet from galloping down the hall like those of a spooked horse. But by the time she reached her locker, her Urban Decay mascara was dribbling down her face. She quickly opened her locker and threw her flash cards on the top shelf, then grabbed her favorite Salvation Army jean jacket and slammed the door shut.

"You never said what time the car wash started."

Marnie sneered at Weston, hoping this would be a

big enough hint that she didn't want to talk to or look at him.

"Who cares? No one is going to come anyway," Marnie said.

"They will if I decide to go," Weston replied. "I may be new to PoCen, but it seems as though I've got more clout than you these days."

Marnie spun around with the intention of telling Weston to shove his clout where the sun didn't shine, but when she saw his gorgeous, rosy-cheeked face and his dark red lips, all she could do was say, "Huh?"

"Listen, I know you're kind of short on friends right now." Weston flexed the brim of his Red Sox hat and smiled. "Why else would you refuse the easy out I gave you with Mrs. Robertson?"

Marnie turned to her locker and opened it, shoving books into her bag ferociously. "I just felt sorry for you, that's all," she lied.

"How funny. I'm going to help you with this fund-raiser for the exact same reason," Weston said as he leaned on the locker next to Marnie's.

"Well, it's a better reason than trying to *get in my pants*," Marnie said sarcastically.

Weston laughed. "Oh, I couldn't disagree more, bud."

Marnie slammed her locker door shut and narrowed her eyes at Weston, preparing to slug him, when she saw Lizette Levin over his shoulder. With Weston as her shield, Marnie observed Lizette carefully as she approached the school's front doors while checking her watch. Perhaps Lizette was about to have a rendezvous with a certain slimeball! Marnie had to find out the truth, with or without her mother's opera glasses.

"Hold my stuff," she said, shoving her bag into Weston's hands.

"Wait, where are you going?" Weston asked, baffled.

"Just stay put, okay? I'll be right back."

Once Marnie saw Lizette leave the building, she charged down the hallway like a panther. Then she propped the front door open so she could catch a glimpse of where Lizette was headed. (Luckily, Lizette was wearing a pair of crossing-guard-orange leggings underneath her mod-print sweater shift dress, so she was easy to spot from a distance.) Marnie's eyes stayed glued to Lizette as she wandered down the hill on the main path. Marnie scampered out the door, taking extreme caution as she trailed her target and ducked behind shrubbery and trees. Lizette was walking quite slowly due to the sky-high stiletto booties she was wearing, so Marnie didn't even lose her breath or break a sweat.

Until Marnie's ex-kinda-sorta-boyfriend entered the picture.

Marnie gasped when Lizette glided toward Dane, who was sitting on the hood of his prized cobalt-blue Jag, smiling arrogantly. He straightened his hay-colored tweed jacket before pulling Lizette into an ultratight hug that lasted way too long.

Marnie gritted her teeth and clenched her jaw.

How could she?! After all her talk about loyalty*?!*

Marnie was about to jump out from behind a thick patch of bushes and yell "Ah ha!" when someone else came on the scene. Marnie recognized the guy from Student Council — Andrew Leshinsky, junior-class vice president and high-ranking Major. Brown-haired and green-eyed, Andrew was over six feet tall, the star forward on the varsity basketball team, and heir to a sizable fortune, which his father had amassed as a day trader. Andrew was, to put it mildly, the mac daddy of the junior boys.

Dane let go of Lizette so he could knock fists with Andrew in a show of Major solidarity. Then Marnie saw something that knocked her on her butt — literally.

Andrew edged by Dane, cupped Lizette's face in his hands, and kissed her. Not a friendly "how do you do?" kiss, either. It was a lip-licking, tongue-wiggling, stomach-churning spectacle that ruled out any Dane/

Lizette tryst. Now that Marnie thought a bit harder, Andrew certainly matched the description Lizette had given her a few weeks ago — he was both an upperclassman *and* a Leek. Too bad Lizette had never mentioned that her super crush was *a freaking basketball player*! Maybe then Marnie wouldn't be lying on the grass like an idiot.

Marnie brushed herself off and stood up slowly as Lizette and Andrew piled into Dane's car. Lizette rode shotgun while Andrew managed to paw at her from the backseat. This could explain how the bracelet had ended up on the floor of Dane's car. Even if it didn't, Lizette was obviously innocent of cheating, and charges should therefore be dropped.

As Marnie walked back toward the school, she reminded herself that she was innocent, too. But that didn't matter. Brynne Callaway and her spy had made sure of it.

Chapter 12

Nola was highly jittery and excitable during Friday morning's homeroom. In approximately thirty-four hours, she and Matt were going to be sitting at a table together at Milanese, eating chicken parmesan and staring lovingly at each other while a violin quartet serenaded them. Okay, so most of those details were a product of Nola's vivid imagination, but she was pretty sure that there was a good chance of chicken parmesan being on the menu at an Italian restaurant. The rest would take care of itself, wouldn't it?

Nola glanced over at Matt, who was in the back of the classroom helping Sawyer Lee out with some sort of tech problem. Matt tinkered with Sawyer's green iPod, his fingers dancing swiftly along the circular pad while he spoke. Nola couldn't hear what Matt was saying, but it didn't matter. She'd become so familiar with the way his lips moved that she could probably piece his words together by just watching his mouth from afar. However, when Nola zoomed in on Matt's succulent lips and saw them move in a way that could only form one word, she shuddered.

Riley. He'd just said, "Riley."

Nola balled up her hands into fists and pulled them inside her sweater sleeves. At first, she wanted to slug Matt for asking her on this ridiculous "warm-up date" and sending her hopes flying. Then once reason set in, she wanted to deck herself for being such a dolt. What was it going to take to get her over Matt? Did she have to exile herself to the Sudan or something even more extreme? Nola wasn't sure. But one thing remained certain — regardless of how close she and Matt became or how many secrets they shared, he still had a freaking *girlfriend*!

Nola sighed. It was pointless to be so hung up on Matt, who was obviously emotionally unavailable, when there was a nice boy who *liked* her and wasn't attached. There was also the option of a moody college guy who had dared to kiss her and tell her she was beautiful. Forgetting about Matt should have been easy with all these eligible hot guys after her, shouldn't it?

But when Nola felt Matt's sweet breath tickle the back of her neck and his soft, cool cheek press up against hers, she knew that she wouldn't be able to forget about Matt, even if she came down with amnesia.

"Looking forward to tomorrow night," Matt said. "What about you?"

Nola couldn't figure out whether she wanted to turn around and plant a huge passionate kiss on Matt or poke him in the eyes. So she just stayed still and nodded.

The P.A. began to blare, and a blustery, unkempt Miss Lucas straightened her misbuttoned blouse and shouted something that sounded like "Shut up!" Matt, Nola, and the rest of the students took that as their cue to take their seats and settle down.

"Good morning, Poughkeepsie Central. We'd like to start off Friday's announcements with the Homecoming court lists. We'll begin with the freshman class girls."

Nola slunk down in her seat a little bit. She knew there was no chance she'd hear her name called, and it kind of hurt to feel like that.

"Brynne Callaway."

Nola could hear some girls squealing and applauding, but she didn't bother checking to see who they were. Mostly because if the Almighty Lizette Levin caught Nola looking in her direction for a fraction of a nanosecond, she'd do something unnecessarily mean and ensure Nola would regret it.

"Grier Hopkins."

A few hoots and whistles sounded throughout the room. Nola chuckled in amusement. This list of Homecoming nominees was so unshocking, it was almost comical. Nola and everyone else at the school knew whose name was going to come next.

"Lizette Levin."

Nola peeked over her shoulder slowly to get a glimpse of Lizette's false-as-pleather reaction, but as usual Lizette was late for homeroom.

After one more freshman girl was nominated for Homecoming court, five boys' names were read off one by one. Not surprisingly, too-hot-for-his-own-good-and-the-safety-of-others Weston Briggs had managed to claim a spot on the list. Matt cheered when Sawyer Lee's name boomed out of the loudspeaker.

Then a crackling noise could be heard, which sounded like a rustling of paper. After a brief pause, a slightly wavering voice said:

"We accidentally omitted a name from the freshman girls' Homecoming list. Congratulations to Marnie Fitzpatrick. You are also honored with a nomination."

Nola joined the rest of her classmates in a collective gasp.

Marnie is on the freshman Homecoming court?!

Considering all the whispering that commenced, nobody could believe that after the harsh anti-Marnie decree that Lizette and the Majors had sent down to the rest of the Minors, Wannabes, and so on, Marnie would be able to secure a place on the list. Nola recalled the day when they had to cast their ballots and everyone was gossiping about how Marnie wouldn't win any popularity votes this time. She just couldn't understand how her ex-friend always managed to pull off the impossible, and a wave of jealousy ripped through her.

For the next few minutes, Nola listened to the rest of the Homecoming court nominations as the chatter from her classmates overlapped into one big cacophony. The bell rang and everyone scampered out of the room, but Nola lagged behind. When Matt stopped at the door and noticed she wasn't walking out with him, he mouthed, "You okay?"

Nola didn't quite know how to answer that, so she just shrugged. Matt squinted at her as though he was trying to surmise whether or not he should press her, but then he looked at the clock on the wall. Matt pointed at it and frowned, indicating that he had to go to class. Nola smiled, feeling comforted by Matt's friendliness, and waved good-bye to him.

Once Matt was gone, Nola gathered up her things and tried to put her anger aside. But her efforts were futile. Nola shoved her math and English textbooks into her book bag so hard that she nearly tore a hole in the tough corduroy fabric. When she slung it over her shoulder, she thought about hurling it into space. It just wasn't fair that when bad stuff happened to Marnie, she still came out smelling like a bouquet of red roses.

The hallway was empty. Instead of heading to class, Nola dawdled and returned to her locker for a new ballpoint pen. She was about to scurry off when she saw Marnie near her locker being cornered by a monumentally pissed-off Lizette, who was flanked by Brynne and Grier.

Nola ducked behind a nearby wall in an adjacent corridor so she wouldn't be seen. She poked her head out just enough to watch Marnie grapple with the girls whom Nola had detested from the first day of school.

"I want to know what kind of trick you pulled, and I want to know *now*!" Lizette barked. Her hands were planted firmly on her glittery genie-pants-clad hips as Brynne and Grier stood at attention behind her, their identical short skirts and tall riding boots making them look like twins.

Nola saw Marnie wrap her arms around herself protectively, as though she was waiting for a mob to beat up on her. Even so, Marnie didn't back down.

"I didn't pull *any* trick, Zee. I was just as surprised about my nomination as you are," Marnie replied.

"Why should we believe you, liar?" Brynne chided as she stepped in front of Lizette and got in Marnie's face.

Nola felt the skin on her neck start to burn like charcoal. She didn't think that after everything that had gone down, she could actually still be scared for Marnie.

"*Don't* call me a liar, *bitch*!" Marnie spat.

Nola almost let out a holler and rooted for Marnie, so she clamped both her hands over her mouth.

But Brynne just cackled as a worried Grier and a pleased Lizette looked on. "I may be a bitch, but at least I don't spend my time *following* people around like a lowlife stalker."

Nola cringed as Marnie's courage faded from her bright blue eyes.

"Brynne's spy saw you trailing Zee yesterday," Grier said tersely. "And we didn't like hearing about it one bit."

There are spies at this high school?! Nola was utterly flabbergasted.

Marnie lowered her head. "I'm sorry, Zee. I just thought —"

"What? That you could play *tag-along* with my *shadow*?" Lizette jabbed Marnie in the shoulder with a sharp index finger. "Get a freaking life!"

Brynne started laughing so hard, she almost fell on the floor. "Oh, my god, Zee. You are the best!"

Nola knew she should be elated to watch Marnie burn at the stake, but she wasn't.

"Come on, guys. I don't want to get written up," whined Grier. The nervousness in her voice seemed to indicate that she also didn't want to witness this cruelty any longer.

Lizette cocked her head to the side and spun around without saying another word. But Brynne wasn't about to miss the opportunity to offer some departing advice to Marnie.

"Do everyone a favor, okay, Fatty? Skip the Homecoming dance," Brynne sneered. "Nobody wants you there, and besides, your sister will be chilling with us anyway."

Nola didn't get a chance to see Marnie's reaction. As soon as she realized Lizette, Brynne, and Grier were parading down the hallway, Nola quickly smashed her back up against the wall so her presence wouldn't be detected. Once she was in the clear, Nola leaned out a little farther and gaped at Marnie as she dashed toward the front doors of the school.

Marnie's heart-wrenching sobs echoed in Nola's ears for the rest of the day. But she never expected that when she went home and settled back into the quiet solitude of her room she'd feel sorry for the girl who had made her cry so many times before.

Chapter 13

If someone had told Marnie two weeks ago that she would be spending a Friday night watching *Spice Up My Kitchen* with her mother, she would have laughed, if not guffawed. But here she was, snuggled underneath her grandmother's homemade patchwork afghan and curled up on the love seat while her mom sat in her father's favorite chair, plunging her hand into a bowl of Cheetos cheese puffs. After what had happened that morning, who could blame Marnie for wanting to veg in front of the TV and watch home improvement shows until her brain turned into a hot pile of goop?

However, after two hours of watching small, rustic kitchens being transformed into modern, sleek eat-ins, Marnie's mind had not been remotely goopified. In fact, her memory files were hard at work, flooding all her synapses with images like a Kodak Gallery online slide show. Not only was Marnie severely sore from the verbal slug-fest that happened at school (she'd spent the entire day with Nurse Mulchahy) but she also couldn't forget all the good times she and Lizette had shared. Whether they were carousing at the Galleria or hanging out at Grier's illustrious crib or gossiping at the coolest parties, when Marnie was with Lizette, she always felt like a better version of herself. But now she was virtually a nobody, and the fear of being a social leper for the next four years was taking hold of her more and more each day. In fact, she would have been crying right now if her tear ducts hadn't dried out that afternoon.

If all that mental anguish wasn't enough, Marnie was constantly thinking about Dane and Sawyer, too. Actually, it hadn't quite sunk in yet that Marnie wouldn't be going to Homecoming with either of them . . . or at all, for that matter. There was no way she'd risk showing up at PoCen's biggest social event now.

During a commercial break, Marnie pulled the afghan up to her chin and tried to imagine what it might feel like to be crowned freshman class Homecoming queen.

"*Mooooooom!* Have you seen my patent-leather T-straps? I need them for tonight!" Erin's voice boomed from upstairs.

And just like that, Marnie decided it was better to be ignorant about such things, especially when Homecoming queens came in the form of her evil older sister.

Mrs. Fitzpatrick's eyes stayed glued on the flickering light of the TV as she shouted, "No, sweetie. Maybe Marnie knows where they are."

"She better not!" Erin yelled as she flounced down the stairs.

Marnie rolled her eyes. Now more than ever, she believed that her life depended on ditching the Homecoming dance. If she had to witness the entire school bowing down to her prima donna sister, she just might go into a frenzy and burn down the gymnasium, *Carrie*-style.

When Erin appeared in the doorway, wearing a silver pleated tube dress from Bebe and a scowl on her face, Marnie immediately pulled the afghan over her head. Problem was, the afghan was made of a very loose weave, so she could still see Erin's pout clear as day.

"I don't know where your shoes are, Erin, so leave me alone," Marnie said.

"What*ever*. I'm running late and don't have time for your *juvenile* games," Erin scoffed.

Oh, please.

"Where are you going, honey?" Mrs. Fitzpatrick asked brightly.

Suddenly, Erin flashed an effervescent grin. "Oh, there is this off-the-heizezy soiree at Alicia Blair's house. All of last year's seniors will be there."

"How fun!" Mrs. Fitzpatrick grabbed the remote and shut off the TV with great excitement so she could give her daughter her undivided attention. "What about Gage Fisher? Will he be there?"

"Ohmigod, I hope so. I look *hella-fabulous* tonight," Erin said, twirling around so her skirt fluttered.

"He'll die when he sees you," Mrs. Fitzpatrick affirmed.

Good, hopefully Erin will die, too.

Marnie's smart-ass interior monologue must have showed up on her mom's radar because Mrs. Fitzpatrick got up from her chair and quickly pulled the afghan off of Marnie's head, sending a shot of static electricity through Marnie's already knotty hair.

"I have a great idea," Mrs. Fitzpatrick said while pinching one of Marnie's cheeks. "Erin, why don't you take Marnie to your party?"

Erin's and Marnie's mouths dropped open in unison.

"Mom, you can't be serious," Erin blurted out after the initial shock wore off.

Mrs. Fitzpatrick tugged at the elastic on her bright indigo J. Jill sweatpants and gaped at Erin. "I am serious. You two should have some sisterly bonding time together and Alicia's party sounds —"

"Off-limits! I can't bring her there, Mom. No underclassmen are allowed," Erin said.

Marnie's heart fluttered. *No underclassmen allowed?* Without the threat of her freshman foes, Marnie might be able to stun the world and redeem her rep at this exclusive party — if she worked her goods hard enough.

"Well, I'm sure Alicia will make an exception for you. Besides, Marnie needs all the good press she can get," Mrs. Fitzpatrick said, winking.

"Very funny," Marnie replied.

Erin stomped her foot as though she were a five-year-old having a hissy fit. "Ugh, fine! Just hurry up and get ready."

And with that vote of confidence, Marnie flew off the couch and galloped up the stairs as fast as she could.

An hour and a half later, Marnie was jammed into the crowded living room of Alicia Blair's luxury condo with her sister and a swarm of Poughkeepsie Central's hottest alumni. This soiree was unlike any party Marnie had attended with Dane or Lizette, and not only because most of the guests were college freshmen. It was as though Marnie had snuck into some exclusive magazine-sponsored Academy Awards after-party. Alicia was handing out gift bags to everyone who crossed the threshold of her posh home (which looked like it had been decorated by Nate Berkus). Each person who strolled by Marnie with a freshly made cocktail looked as though they'd gotten dressed with the assistance of a personal stylist. The lights were dim, the music was thumping, and all Marnie wanted to do was . . . get the hell out of there.

For the last twenty minutes, Erin had been juggling the infamous Gage Fisher (who could be best described as a yummy blend of all three Jonas Brothers) and a ditzy sorority girl who laughed/coughed like she had a black lung. As for Marnie, she had been pressed up against the wall near a red-and-blue Marla Olmstead painting, wondering why she'd even bothered to wear her killer outfit. No one had noticed Marnie or her jade Ella Moss ruffle-yoke tee or her hippie-inspired flare-leg jeans from TopShop. And try as she might, Marnie couldn't get in touch with her assertive, bubbly personality and talk to any of Erin's friends.

Marnie didn't think she'd ever understand what Nola was going through at Lizette's murder-mystery party, but now she could really relate.

Erin peeked over Gage's shoulder and spied Marnie cowering near the painting. She made a distressed face and excused herself from their conversation, then skimmed through the throngs of bodies so she could impress upon Marnie just how displeased she was.

"God, could you be acting any weirder?" Erin snapped before taking a sip from a large glass with a lime wedge on the rim.

"I'm not acting weird, I'm . . . scoping out the scene," Marnie said defensively. "By the way, thanks for *not* introducing me to any of your crew. I feel like I fit right in."

"Hey, I didn't tell Mom I'd introduce you at the party. I just said I'd *bring* you," Erin said with a smirk.

Marnie shook her head in amazement. "Gee, that's awfully helpful of you, big sis."

"Don't give me that. I've helped you plenty since I've been home," Erin said, spinning around so she could people-watch with Marnie.

"Are you kidding me? When?"

"Have you forgotten all the kick-ass tips I gave you regarding your unfortunate situation?"

"They've been *far* from kick-ass, Erin. And I have nothing to show for it."

"Yeah, you do." Erin elbowed Marnie in the ribs and winked. "You got nominated to the Homecoming court."

Ohmigod! She didn't*!*

Marnie lunged at Erin and grabbed hold of her sister's arms. "*Pleeeeease* tell me you had nothing to do with getting me nominated for freshman Homecoming queen."

When Erin grinned, her teeth and tongue were as blue as the mixed drink in her glass. "You should be *thanking* me!"

"Ugh!" Marnie wanted to shake Erin until her head popped off, but she let go of her sister and angrily shoved her hands in her pockets. "Why should I *thank* you? Lizette and Brynne almost dug out my spleen when they heard I was nominated. Now they think I'm trying to challenge them or something!"

Erin shrugged. "So what? If you're crowned queen, you'll have leverage against the both of them. Then you can start calling the shots. Isn't that what you want?"

Marnie's head was spinning. Why did it always feel like she had to strategize like a politician when Lizette was involved?

"What I want is some fresh air," she said sharply.

"Whatever," Erin replied without a hint of concern. Then she snaked through the crowd and sidled up next to Gage.

Marnie squeezed her way through the living room until she finally reached a set of French doors, which led to the patio. She sighed in relief when she realized they were unlocked and quietly slid into the brisk night air. Marnie shivered a little when she closed the doors — she probably should have snagged her jacket.

"Stay out here too long and you'll catch a cold." A voice sounded from behind the shadows.

Marnie leaned forward a bit and saw a trail of smoke floating up into the starry sky. "Sawyer?"

As soon as he stepped out into the moonlight, Marnie could see Sawyer Lee and his silver puffer coat plain as day.

He took another drag from his cigarette and said, "In the flesh."

Marnie had to fold her hands together to prevent them from shaking. "What are you doing here?"

"My older brother, Christian, is Alicia's boyfriend." Sawyer's smile wavered like a flickering candle. "He thought I should do some hobnobbing, but I ended up on the patio all night."

Marnie grinned. She thought she'd be enjoying this party as well, but only now was she beginning to relax and have fun.

"Are you sure you don't want to run in the other direction? Someone might see us together and go tell Zee," Sawyer said as he stomped out his cigarette with his Vans.

Ow.

Marnie ignored his sarcasm and rubbed her arms to keep herself warm. "No, I like it out here."

“I’d offer to give you my jacket, but you know what happened last time,” Sawyer joked.

“That’s okay. I’m fine.”

“If you’re fine, then why aren’t you inside?”

Marnie glanced up and watched a dark cloud pass by. “I don’t know. Maybe I was . . . overwhelmed.”

Sawyer ran his hand over his stubbly scalp. “By what?”

Marnie hesitated. What Sawyer had said about someone seeing them together triggered a fear inside Marnie that she just couldn’t quell. But when Marnie locked eyes with him, she wanted to tell him everything.

“By *life,*” she blurted out, her voice cracking unexpectedly. “I came here tonight hoping that it would, like, resurrect my rep, but instead I feel like such an outsider.”

“I hate to say it, but I don’t know why anyone would want to be *insiders* with those fools.” Sawyer rolled his eyes. “What’s the point of being friends with people who are going to turn on you at the drop of a hat?”

The French doors opened a crack and a handsome-looking Asian guy poked his head out and shouted, “Dude, there you are. I want to introduce you to somebody.”

Sawyer waved him off as if to say, *I’ll be right there.*

“Is that Christian?” Marnie asked.

“What gave it away?” Sawyer said with a wink.

Marnie laughed and the outline of her breath became visible. “I guess I’ll see you around.”

“Hope so.” Sawyer gave her a half grin and then returned to the party.

Marnie would have followed him, too, if she had been stronger.

Chapter 14

Late Saturday afternoon, Iris Santos showed up at Nola's house without warning, holding a huge crate of supplies that she referred to as her Makeover Machine. Apparently, Matt had accidentally let it slip to his other female confidante that he was taking Nola out tonight. According to Iris, no woman should get ready for a date — warm-up or otherwise — all by herself. Nola, of course, had no choice but to agree.

After an hour of fighting over Nola's outfit (Nola was adamant about wearing something in the pants family, like khakis or jeans, while Iris insisted that Nola "flash some leg-candy" in a cute miniskirt), they had compromised on a gold fitted tunic top from Miss Sixty and a black knee-length skirt paired with grape-colored L.A.M.B. oxford pumps. The machine was also filled with a slew of accessories — belts, barrettes, hosiery, etc. — which they still needed to wade through. But for now, Nola was sitting on the edge of her bed in her Gap Body pale blue cotton bra and panties as Iris attempted to do Nola's hair and makeup.

"Would you stop wiggling around so much? I don't know how you expect me to apply eyeliner when you're seizing like that," Iris harrumphed as she drew a fine streak of purple underneath Nola's eyelid.

"Well, maybe I wouldn't be seizing if a pencil wasn't *near my eyeball,*" Nola said, covering her bare belly with her arms and looking up to the ceiling. "I'd also be a lot more comfortable if I wasn't half naked."

Iris snickered while tossing the eyeliner into a plastic see-through cosmetics bag and picking up a Stila smoky eye palette compact with four shimmering shadows in it. "It's just us girls, Nola. What are you being so prudish about?"

"I'm *not* a prude," Nola muttered. Iris just didn't comprehend how anxious Nola was over . . . pretty much everything these days.

"All right, spill." Iris yanked up her tangerine-colored lounge pants at the knees, kicked off her flip-flops, and plopped down on Nola's carpet.

"Spill what?"

"There's something bothering you."

"How can you tell?" Nola asked as she bit off a hangnail.

"Because you're being much more annoying than usual," Iris replied.

"*I'm* being annoying?"

"Yeah, you. I came over here to turn you into a glamour-puss, which is supposed to be — *duh* — fun!

And all you are giving me is a load of grief," Iris explained. "So what gives?"

Nola would have hidden her face behind her hands, but she didn't want to wreck all the work Iris had already done to her eyes. So instead she fell backward on her bed. That way Iris wouldn't be able to see the blotches that were starting to form near her earlobes. Nola wished that she could open up to Iris about all of her worries. She really needed a friend right now.

But that was just the problem. Ever since she'd seen Marnie get annihilated by Lizette yesterday, Nola couldn't get her ex-friend off of her mind. For weeks Nola had been livid about how Marnie had treated her, but over the last twenty-four hours that rage had given way to sadness. Maybe it was because she realized for the first time just how hard Marnie was getting punished for something Nola knew in her heart-of-hearts Marnie would never do. Or perhaps a part of Nola that still thought fondly of Marnie was reignited when she watched Marnie stand up for herself and tell Brynne off.

Regardless of the reason, Nola missed Marnie more today than she had the entire time they'd switched from being best friends to sworn enemies. In fact, while Iris had been busy fussing with the contents of her Makeover Machine, Nola had been thinking about how

Marnie should have been helping her prep for tonight. Unlike Iris, Marnie would have known just how much Nola hated putting on heavy makeup, and while she'd encourage Nola to show a bit of skin, Marnie would have jokingly coaxed Nola in that special way of hers that made Nola's stress disappear.

However, Iris had her own brand of coaxing, and it involved bouncing up from the floor and pinching Nola on her upper thigh.

"Yeow!" Nola shouted out in pain.

"Hey, I was just snapping you back to reality, girl," Iris said, smiling so Nola could see the glint of her silver braces.

Nola rubbed the dark pink welt Iris had left on her skin. "Gee, thanks."

Iris parked herself next to Nola and swept her bangs to the right of her forehead. "Listen, Nola, I know I'm not Marnie. But straight up, you can talk to me about whatever is bugging you out. I can be a good listener when I shut my trap, honest."

Nola's demeanor immediately softened. The one thing that Nola always appreciated about Iris was her honesty, even when it hurt — literally. Maybe confiding in her was the right thing to do.

Nola ran her hands through her hair and took a deep breath. "Well, I'm —"

"Nervous about playing tonsil hockey with Evan at Homecoming?" Iris interrupted enthusiastically.

So much for shutting her trap.

Nola cleared her throat and tried again. "Actually, it's more like —"

"Nervous about playing tonsil hockey with Matt tonight?"

Nola threw her hands up in the air and yelled, "Enough with the tonsil hockey already!"

"Well, excuse me! I just happen to be sensing a strong kissing-angst vibe emanating from this room," Iris said, offended.

Nola swallowed hard and her fingers went numb. *Kissing-angst vibe?* This *room? How did —*

"Ohmigod! Your upper lip is sweating. I knew it! You *do* have kissing angst!" Iris tousled Nola's hair like a little kid.

"No, I don't," Nola said, her voice squeaky.

Iris stared Nola down. "You want to mess with the debate team master?"

"No, I don't," Nola said, her voice even squeakier.

"Okay, I'll go easy on you." Iris giggled. "What do you want to know about kissing?"

What Nola really wanted to know was *why* a certain annoying college student/child-care provider had given her a mind-blowing kiss to begin with. Was it just curiosity? Had he been huffing aerosol paint cans? Or did Ian Capshaw have genuine feelings for her?

Regardless of the reason, this kiss had certainly jarred their relationship out of alignment. Since the brusque kitchen incident, Ian had been lying low and avoiding contact with Nola as much as possible. In fact, Ian was currently downstairs watching Nola's brothers and he hadn't intruded on Nola and Iris once. Strange, indeed.

Still, Nola knew that she wouldn't hear the end of it if she told Iris about her kiss with Ian. So she had to use the utmost finesse.

Keep it vague, Nol. Very, very vague.

"When someone kisses you, does it . . . always mean that they *like* you?"

Iris's brow furrowed. "*Hmmm.* Good question. Lots of romantic twits would say yes, but my verdict is no. Sometimes, a kiss is just a kiss, you know? Hormones are raging and things happen."

Nola felt a prickle of disappointment travel down her spine. While she wasn't sure how she felt about Ian, it wasn't easy for Nola to accept that their romantic moment may have been just a random glitch.

"Why? Who did you kiss? Was it Evan? Was it *Matt*?!" Iris was practically hyperventilating.

"Don't you think you would have pried it out of me by now if I had kissed *either* of them?"

"Good point." Iris rubbed her chin, contemplating her next guess. "Wait a second. Was it —"

All of a sudden, Nola's door flew open and there stood Ian, his nose buried in the same book from the other day. Nola screamed the moment she saw him mindlessly enter her room. Ian was so caught off-guard that when he glanced up, he almost tripped over his own feet. Nola grabbed the quilt off her bed and tried to wrap it around her midsection before Ian caught a glimpse of her undies. But from the tint of Ian's bright red cheeks, it was clear that she was too late.

As for Iris, she just stood back and watched the comedy unfold while attempting to hold in her laughter.

"Whatareyoudoinginhere?! Areyouinsane?! Ican't believeyou!!" Nola shrieked.

Ian plugged his ears with his fingers until Nola paused to inhale. "I'm sorry!" he exclaimed. "I wasn't paying attention. I thought I was opening the door to the bathroom!"

I. Am. Going. To. KILL. HIM!

"Oh, I'll make sure you pay attention from now on," Nola said, lunging at Ian with both hands while holding the quilt tightly underneath her armpits.

Iris stepped in front of Nola and saved Ian from a grisly death. "Nola's just a little tense, Ian. You caught her at a bad time."

Ian continued to blush. "I know! I know! I feel like such a —"

"*Pervert?!*" Nola barked.

Slowly the stunned expression on Ian's face turned into a wounded one and Nola's stomach lurched. Even Iris, who was the queen of bold statements and borderline-aggressive remarks, shook her head at Nola in disapproval. Why did she lose her temper so quickly around Ian? He obviously had just made a mistake. There was no real reason to fly off the handle. Unless her feelings for Ian ran deeper than she thought.

"Nola, that was a low blow," Iris said as she sashayed over to Ian and stood by his side. "I think you should apologize."

Nola gripped the quilt with her fingertips, the sting of humiliation still fresh on her body. "Sorry, Ian."

But Ian just stood there, motionless.

Iris punched him in the shoulder lightly. "Never mind Nola. She's all worked up about her hot date tonight. You know how it is, right, Ian? All those college girls throwing themselves at you every day and —"

"You're going on a *date*?" Ian interjected, his eyebrows reaching up into a high arch.

Oh, great. Here we go!

"It's not really a date," Nola began to explain.

"What is it, then? And who is it with?" Ian took a step toward Nola, but Iris blocked his path.

"Ian, I think one of the twins just got hit with a mallet. You better make sure there's no permanent brain damage done," she said, crossing her arms across her chest.

Seeing that he wasn't going to get past Iris, Ian shoved his book in his back pocket and marched out, sighing heavily as he shut the door behind him.

"Holy crap! YOU. KISSED. IAN!" Iris had no idea how loud she was being, which was why Nola dropped her quilt and socked Iris with a pillow.

"*Shhhh!!!!* He'll hear you!!!" Nola whispered. "And *I* didn't kiss *him*. *He* kissed *me*."

"Even better!" Iris snatched the pillow out of Nola's grasp and bopped Nola on the butt with it. "You could cut the sexual tension in here with a butter knife. And did you see how *jealous* he got when he heard you were going on a date? Girl, you are *so* babe-a-licious!"

"I'm not babe-a-licious and he's not jealous. Can't you see the only reason Ian kissed me was because he had some sort of . . . psychotic break?"

"Psychotic break, my ass," Iris said. "When are you going to get it through your thick skull that when you're not being all brooding and self-conscious, you're actually pretty?"

Nola approached the full-length mirror that stood in the corner of her room and studied her face and figure. She never thought of herself as unattractive, but she never thought of herself as pretty, either. Still, it was hard to ignore what Iris had just said, especially when there seemed to be a few boys (and a slimeball, too) who were attracted to Nola's unique brand of beauty. Not that she cared what any of them thought, but the attention did seem to validate what an ex-friend had been telling her all along.

"You really think so?"

Iris came up behind Nola and she saw the reflection of Iris's smile. "It only matters what Matt thinks, right?"

Nola rolled her eyes at Iris, who retreated to her Makeover Machine. But try as she might, Nola couldn't stop wishing for Matt to realize that they were meant to be together, no matter how many times it led to disappointment.

Then again, there was a full moon in Poughkeepsie tonight. Another surprise kiss could be just around the corner.

Chapter 15

The staff parking lot of Poughkeepsie Central was completely bare late Saturday afternoon, with the exception of Marnie, Weston, two buckets of soapy water, and two containers of Turtle Wax. For the past three hours, Marnie had been holding up a sign that read, COME SUPPORT THE FRESHMAN CLASS CAR WASH! and plastering a wide smile on her face every time a minivan, SUV, compact, or sedan whooshed down the street. Not one lousy person took the bait — even a filthy flatbed truck with an inch worth of caked-on grime clinging to the windshield zoomed by Marnie as if she weren't there.

Which was par for the course these days.

"Maybe you should have worn something a little more flashy. You know, like the *Maxim* cover girls do," Weston said snidely as he sat in a fold-up beach chair, his legs spread wide apart. Instead of helping Marnie lure customers to her hopelessly tragic fund-raiser, he'd spent his time tossing a baseball up in the air and catching it. As well as dispensing insightful observations such as this.

"Yeah, well, maybe you should have used your 'clout' and brought all your 'peeps,' like you said you were going to." Marnie examined her Gap khaki-and-hoodie outfit to see if it was cute enough, but then caught herself. Why was she even *listening* to Weston anyway?

"My clout is nothing compared to Lizette's," Weston said, readjusting his Red Sox cap so Marnie could see more of his beaming blue eyes. "Yesterday morning, I'd convinced an army of freshmen to come, but by seventh period, they had all talked to Brynne. I guess we're witnessing the aftermath, huh?"

Marnie successfully quelled a piteous moan that was building up inside her chest. "I guess."

"So why don't we just bag this thing and go do something else?" Weston asked.

Marnie rolled her eyes. "We have earned *zero* dollars. ZERO! I am class *treasurer*. If the freshmen don't contribute financially to the Homecoming dance, *I'm* to blame. The student council board will probably impeach me or something!"

Marnie was too rattled to care about how crazy and unhinged she sounded. But when she saw a navy blue Volvo in close range, Marnie was so desperate for a customer, she jumped up and down with the sign held high above her head and shouted, "Free car wash! FREE CAR WASH!"

The Volvo slowed down, which sent Marnie's hopes

soaring, but it eventually turned the corner and drove away.

"I admire your salesmanship, Marnie. Coaxing the first patron in with a free car wash isn't a bad idea," Weston said, stretching his arms out in front of him.

"Shut up, Weston." Marnie tossed the sign into the air. Once it fluttered down to the asphalt, she sat on top of it, crossed her legs, and placed her elbows on her knees. "I should just give in already. Resign my post and register at a religious commune charter school."

Weston jammed his baseball into the pocket of his olive-colored cargo pants and leaned back in his chair so it was teetering on its back legs. "Come on, Marnie. Your life isn't that bad."

Marnie cocked her head to the side and gave Weston a sarcastic look.

"Okay, it *is* that bad," Weston said as he plunged his hand into a bucket of water and pulled out a soaking-wet sponge. "But I'm still here, right?"

Marnie scratched at her temple. "Right . . . but why?"

"You're my buddy, remember?" Weston's amazing smile cracked open and he let out a loud yet friendly laugh. "And because I wanted to see what would happen when I did . . . THIS!"

Weston shook the sponge really hard so that sprays of water flew directly at Marnie. After she yelped in surprise and leaped up, Weston got out of his chair and wrung the sponge out, dousing the seat of Marnie's khakis.

"Ohmigod, Weston! Are you *nine*? And . . . retarded?!" Marnie checked to see the amount of damage done to her pants. Alas, it appeared that her bladder had had an unfortunate accident. Marnie was fuming.

Weston, however, was in hysterics and oblivious to Marnie's rage. "Aw, man. That was *classic*!"

Marnie was 2.5 seconds away from dumping an entire pail of water on Weston and seeing whether or not he thought *that* was classic. But the sound of a car pulling into the staff parking lot distracted her from her impromptu ex-boyfriend grudge-match.

"Looks like we have company," Weston said, grinning.

Marnie spun around and saw the car barreling toward her and Weston. When she realized the following, she started crafting her last will and testament in her head:

1) The car in question was a certain cobalt-blue Jaguar convertible.
2) Dane was at the wheel.

3) An unidentified girl who looked like a miniature version of Jada Pinkett Smith was in the passenger seat.
4) Tucked in the backseat were Lizette and junior class VP Andrew Leshinsky.

Holy crappity-crap!

Before Marnie could begin to form some sort of strategy, the Jag came to a halt before her and Weston. Dane put the car in park and revved the engine a few times, causing everyone to cover their ears. Once he was finished goofing around, he turned off the ignition and slung his arm around Mini Jada, who curled up next to him like a hungry boa constrictor. As for Lizette and Andrew, they were shooting Marnie nasty glares.

"Weston Briggs. How goes it?" Dane raised his left hand so Weston could high-five him.

"Oh, it's going much slower than you are, I bet," Weston replied.

Mini Jada giggled and ran her hand up Dane's thigh.

I think I'm going to hurl.

Marnie didn't know what was worse — watching Lizette look right past her, seeing Mini Jada pet Dane like a poodle, or thinking about what would happen if her two ex-boyfriends became . . . friends?

"This car wash fund-raiser was such a *dumb-ass* idea," Lizette said as she ruffled Andrew's caramel-colored hair with her fingers. "No wonder nobody showed up."

"Not everyone can have your brains and beauty, Zee." Andrew planted a soft kiss on Lizette's smiling lips.

"We're going to my house to chill in front of the plasma." Dane put on a pair of Ray-Bans and smirked. "Whaddya say, Briggs? You in?"

Marnie stood there motionless, as though a tranquilizer dart had hit her in the arm. Dane had asked if she was "in" just a few weeks ago, before they went lip-to-lip in the AV room. Did he say this to all the people he wanted to manipulate? From the looks of the girl sitting next to him, the odds were he did.

But at the same time, Marnie remembered how amazing it had felt to be welcomed into Lizette and Dane's exclusive inner circle. Although she was currently being shunned by them, and while Sawyer had given her a lot to think about at Alicia's party, Marnie still wanted to be included. Actually, she *needed* to be included.

Yet what was an excommunicated member of the Majors like her supposed to do? Fall down on her hands and knees and beg for attention? Regardless of how much she envied Weston right now, Marnie wasn't about to humiliate herself so that Lizette and Dane would acknowledge her.

Then again, maybe she didn't even have to try.

"Whoa!" Andrew blurted out as he leaned forward and pointed at Marnie's butt. "Somebody has . . . *issues*."

Lizette craned her neck so she could be in the know. Once she saw the damp circle on the back of Marnie's pants, she practically cackled. "Anyone have a box of ultra-absorbent Depends?"

Marnie closed her eyes and considered walking out into traffic. It was an awful way to die, but no worse than what was happening to her right now.

"There might be some in the trunk," Mini Jada added.

As for Dane, he just covered his mouth and chuckled.

"Easy guys," Weston said. "I splashed Marnie with some water, that's all."

Marnie's eyebrows rose in surprise. Why was Weston sticking up for her? He thrived on watching Marnie squirm!

"Whatever. Just give me a call if you're going to come by." Dane turned the Jag's engine back on and gave Marnie one of his signature glib looks. Then Lizette leaned over the front seat and whispered something into Dane's ear, causing him to break into a loud laugh.

Marnie's skin instantly became sizzling hot as she scolded herself for wanting to chase after them. An emotion she couldn't quite put her finger on hit her like a cyclone. Before she knew what was happening, Marnie snarled at Lizette and Dane, threw her arms around Weston's neck, stood up on her tiptoes, closed her eyes, and kissed him like they were back in the shed behind her house.

Deep in Marnie's subconscious, she was aware that this was a bold, calculated move, meant to show doubters and haters that she was not going down without a serious, knuckle-bleeding fight. However, even Marnie's subconscious was not prepared for a kiss with Weston Briggs. Yes, Marnie had smooched Weston many, many times (she knew she had a numbered list somewhere), but as his amazingly soft mouth moved against hers tenderly, subconscious–Marnie was marveling at how extremely succulent Weston's kisses were. It was a wonder that conscious–Marnie could even pull away.

In fact, the kiss was so heart-stopping that when Marnie opened her eyes, she realized that she hadn't even heard Dane's car pull out of the parking lot and drive down the street, where it was sitting at a stoplight.

"What. Was. *That*?" Weston fell back into his folding chair, completely out of breath and bewildered.

But Marnie didn't answer him. She just splashed some cold, soapy water on her forehead as the Jag spun its wheels and zoomed off when the light turned green.

Chapter 16

It was a chilly and starry night in Poughkeepsie, one that was tailor-made for autumn mischief or romance. As Nola double-timed it down the stairs to get the door, she hoped that even though this was only a practice date, she wouldn't screw it up by saying something dumb or being her usual nervous, klutzy self. Yes, Iris's "you're a knockout in a fashion victim's body" pep talk had definitely given Nola a little ego boost. But the moment Iris had left, Nola took another look in the mirror and what she saw looked more like an imposter.

Nola opened the front door to find Matt on her porch, dressed in a dark gray, ribbed zip-front sweater and clutching a fresh array of peach-colored roses with baby's breath. Nola prayed that her sudden lightheadedness wouldn't lead to a cute-boy-induced stroke.

Matt smiled at Nola, but then he squinted at her as though he couldn't recognize her. "Uh, Nola, what's wrong with your face?"

"Am I breaking out in hives again?" Nola hadn't felt a burning, itchy sensation on her cheeks or chin, but then again, Iris had piled three layers of foundation, blush, eye shadow, lipstick, and various other products on her skin. Maybe all the chemical compounds had numbed her pores.

"No, it's just . . ." Matt took his right thumb and ran it over her lips. Nola's heart performed a free fall into her stomach. "You don't usually wear makeup."

"Well, it's a special occasion. Isn't it?" Nola could swear her teeth were chattering.

"I wouldn't be presenting you with roses if it wasn't." Matt took a gander at her Iris-inspired outfit. "Hey, what's with the glittery top? Are we going to a rave later?"

Now Nola's palms were getting moist. This get-up was supposed to enrapture him, not turn him into Sarcastic Boy. "I just wanted to look nice, that's all."

Matt grinned knowingly. "I have to admit, I've seen that ensemble on Iris before. Did she come over here and do this?"

"Do what?"

"Let her wardrobe throw up on you," Matt said, laughing.

Nola wasn't laughing with him, though. After what she'd been through earlier with Iris and Ian, she didn't want her suffering to be in vain. "I thought one was supposed to dress up for a date."

"Yes, but you're also supposed to look like your wonderful self." Matt handed the flowers to Nola and chuckled. "Why don't you put these in water? Then I'll give you ten minutes to get back to normal." Matt pushed up his sweater sleeve and checked his watch. "Okaaaaay, go!"

Nola brought the flowers up to her nose. "Wow, Matt, these are —"

"Save the compliments for later," he interjected. "We have all night. However, we don't want to be late for our reservations, so . . ." He tapped his watch with his pointer finger.

"Oh, right! I'll be back in a bit," Nola said, smirking.

In a matter of seven or eight minutes, Nola managed to sprint to the kitchen, put the flowers in a vase, run back up to her room, strip down to her underwear, dive into her closet for an alternative date outfit (dark-wash stretch Hudson jeans, a burgundy bell-sleeved shirt, and a pair of brown riding boots), quick change, make a pit stop in the bathroom, wash off two layers of makeup, flip her head over, brush her hair upside down (to achieve maximum volume, naturally), flip back up, gargle with Scope, spritz on some Clinique Happy, and rush down the hall, knocking Dennis (or was it Dylan?) out of the way.

Nola scrambled down the stairs with seconds to spare, but when she arrived at the bottom step she could see that someone had already beaten her to Matt. And that someone was Ian Capshaw.

"So where are you taking her? And when will you be bringing her home?" Ian asked sternly. "I need to keep her parents in the loop."

Nola couldn't have been more humiliated. Was Ian a prison warden in a former life or something?

"First we're going to dinner at Milanese, and after that I'm taking her to the movies," Matt replied cordially. "I don't think we'll be later than eleven."

Ian cracked his knuckles. "You better make it ten."

Okay, that does it!

Nola pegged Ian on the shoulder with her paisley-print hobo bag, causing him to stumble to the side.

"Excuse me, Ian. I'm on my way out," Nola said sharply as she passed him and took Matt's arm. The soft cotton fabric of his sweater felt amazing against her fingertips.

Nola gazed at Matt, forgetting about the false pretense surrounding tonight. "Shall we?"

"We certainly shall," Matt answered, squeezing her hand gently.

When they got to the sidewalk, Matt escorted her to the taxicab that was idling in front of Nola's house. Matt opened the back door and Nola began to get in. But before she could, Matt startled her by grabbing her hand.

"You look stunning, Nola," Matt said sweetly. "Sorry, I couldn't wait until later to tell you."

A broad, toothy smile spread across Nola's face. "Thank you," she said.

Matt smiled back. "And so you know, that wasn't just part of the warm-up."

As she dipped into the cab, Nola felt her ears tingling. Then Matt sat down next to her and the tingling spread to her lips. But the sensation dwindled, just a little, when Nola saw a sad-looking Ian standing on the porch as they drove away.

An hour and a half later, Nola and Matt staggered out of Milanese, giggling. Their faces were a bright shade of red as they held their aching sides. Nola was positive that she'd never laughed this hard in her life. Or felt this good.

"Oh . . . my g-god. Th-that was *awe*some," Matt said, trying to calm down and catch his breath.

"Which part?" Nola wiped at her watery eyes and glanced down at her gravy-stained shirt. "When the waiter dumped your turkey dinner on me? Or when I nearly choked on that piece of ice in my Diet Coke?"

Matt put his hands on his stomach. "Oh, I don't want to play favorites," he said, snickering.

"That's mighty fair of you." Nola picked a fragment of meat off her shoulder and flicked it in Matt's direction.

"Well, I'm as fair as they come, my dear," Matt said, his face glowing in the shroud of moonlight.

Oh, I know.

"And you, Nola, are —"

"A big pathetic mess who ruined our warm-up date?"

Matt clutched at his heart jokingly. "Ow! I wasn't going to say something that mean *and* entirely untrue."

Nola closed in on Matt so she was basking in the same ray of moonlight. "Sorry. What were you going to say?"

"I was going to say" — Matt cleared his throat nervously — "you are very . . . lovely."

Nola tilted her chin down and grinned bashfully.

"And you didn't ruin our warm-up date. Not by a long shot," Matt added.

"That's a relief," Nola said, her hands shaking with elation. "Although I'm afraid to find out what might happen at the movies."

Matt strolled over to Nola and put his arm around her shoulder. "Oh, silly girl. We're not going to the movies."

"We're not?" Nola hoped she didn't sound worried, because in fact she was exhilarated.

"I used the movies as a cover so the General wouldn't get suspicious." Matt patted Nola's back. "Besides, you have to expect the unexpected on your real date with Evan. Why should tonight be any different?"

Nola felt a strong jolt inside her chest. If Matt was mentioning Evan at a time like this, then he probably wasn't taking their date seriously. Then again, Matt hadn't mentioned Riley at all tonight, and that was definitely a step in the right direction.

"Well, where are we going, then?" Nola dared to wrap her arm around Matt and wondered if she'd ever be this comfortable around any other guy.

"To the place where we can best see the stars," Matt said, a hint of romance in his voice. Then he took Nola's hand and beckoned, "This way."

Matt led Nola to a bus stop, where they were lucky enough to catch a ride across town. Twenty minutes later, they hopped off in front of a tall red brick building. Matt walked up to the doorway and pushed a button on the intercom. There was a buzzing sound and Matt pulled the door open for Nola.

"After you, Miss James," he said, smiling.

Nola tucked a strand of hair behind her ear and grinned.

Once they were in the elevator and Matt had selected the button for the top floor, Nola got up the nerve to ask, "Where are we?"

"This is the studio my father records at," Matt explained. "The equipment here is much better than the stuff we have in the attic and there's a lot more room."

"Cool," Nola said. "But I thought —"

Matt tapped Nola on the nose. "Good things come to those who wait, Nol."

Of course, Matt was absolutely right. A minute or two later, the elevator stopped and Matt took Nola onto the building's rooftop, where she could see city lights stretched out for miles. Nola gingerly strolled over to the edge of the roof and observed the Poughkeepsie landscape until Matt stood beside her. Then she stared into his hazel eyes.

"This is amazing," she said breathlessly.

"I know," Matt said with a melancholy sigh. "I come up here a lot when my dad is working late."

Nola pulled her gaze away from Matt and looked up at the sky. "It's a little hard to see the stars, though. Maybe there's too much light from the street."

Matt chuckled. "It's not that hard when you have a telescope."

Nola whipped her head toward Matt. "You have a *telescope?*"

"My mom bought it for me for Christmas when I was seven. I set it up right over there." Matt pointed to a corner of the roof.

Nola spun around and saw a four-foot-long telescope aimed right at the Big Dipper. "Wow!" she exclaimed.

"I guess you wanna try it out, huh?" Matt laughed at Nola's level of enthusiasm.

Nola dashed over to the telescope without even answering Matt. She bent down a little, leaned in, and peered through the eyepiece. Nola didn't have to adjust the focus — the view was spectacular. The glimmering stars seemed so close that she could reach out with her hands and grab hold of hundreds of them.

But before she was able to try, the universe went completely dark. Nola looked up to see what was wrong and saw that Matt was covering the lens with his hand, smirking.

"Do you mind?" Nola said, pretending to be mad.

"Yes, I do. Especially because you're not getting the proper rooftop experience," he replied.

Nola hoped the proper rooftop experience involved their lips.

Matt reached into his back pocket and pulled out his iPod. "You need the right soundtrack."

Nola smiled at Matt, willing him to move closer.

Thankfully, Matt took a few steps toward her, leaving only a small space between them. Nola put in the earbuds while Matt searched for an appropriate song.

"Okay, you can resume your position when you hear the first note." Matt was looking at Nola earnestly, as though he was hoping for something, too.

Nola stayed quiet and attentive, mesmerized by every detail of Matt's face, until the strumming of an acoustic guitar echoed in her ears. Nola knew she was supposed to look through the telescope now, but she couldn't tear her eyes away from Matt, who was still staring at her intensely. As the guitar tempo picked up, a raspy yet soothing voice began to sing. One by one, more instruments chimed in and created an exquisite melody — the low hum of a bass, the slow beat of a drum, and then the wailing screech of an electric guitar, which sounded exactly like a heart breaking.

When the song was over, Nola and Matt stood there gaping at each other, as if they wanted the space between them to disappear.

"You were supposed to look at the stars there," Matt said, breaking their silence but not their eye contact.

"Sorry, I guess the song overpowered me." Nola shivered. It felt like an electrical field was draped above them like a canopy. "What's the name of the band? I really like them."

Matt smiled. "They're in between names at the moment."

Nola gave him a skeptical look. "Really?"

"Yeah, I have it on good authority," Matt replied, his gaze unwavering.

"So what now?" Nola asked.

"I don't know." Matt's chest rose and fell during a deep, deep breath. "The song overpowered me, too."

"But you weren't even listening."

"I was listening, Nol. In my heart."

Matt had just spoken one of those unforgettable movie lines that people quote forever. Nola had already committed it to memory, like she did with most things Matt said. But this time it was different. Tonight, Nola didn't need to read between the lines. She didn't have to make educated guesses about what Matt was thinking.

Because she knew. In her heart. She knew.

Chapter 17

On Sunday morning, Marnie shuffled into the kitchen, fluffy slippers hugging her feet. It was almost noon and the house was quiet. There was the chance that her mother and Erin were still in their rooms. Their doors were closed, so it wasn't a stretch of the imagination to guess that they were sleeping in after a rollicking good time with their respective boy toys.

Of course, Erin had snagged Gage Fisher at Alicia Blair's party on Friday, so on Saturday evening she'd raced off with him in his sleek silver Audi R8 to God knows where. As for Mrs. Fitzpatrick, she went out with a slightly balding, Drew Carey–looking dude from her real estate office. Jake? Jack? Joe? Marnie hadn't cared enough to enter that data into her memory bank once he'd escorted her mom out the door. Most likely because she'd been too busy moping and feeling sorry for herself — fabulous kiss with Weston or no, Marnie's self-esteem was hitting a new low.

Marnie let out a melancholy sigh and went to the refrigerator for some Sunny Delight. She was just about to open the fridge door when she noticed a note addressed to her underneath a lighthouse magnet that Mrs. Fitzpatrick had bought on a family trip to Maine years ago. Marnie removed the magnet so she could take a closer look.

Marnie,
Erin and I went to brunch at the Beech Tree. You were asleep and I didn't want to wake you. We'll be home after we get back from our mani-pedi appointments at Marlene Weber. Hope you are feeling better!
Love,
Mom

Marnie groaned and crumpled up the letter right after she read the phrase "mani-pedi." It was bad enough that she was being avoided like the avian flu at school, but now it was happening at home, too!

Marnie angrily flung open the fridge and grabbed the half-full bottle of Sunny D. She twisted off the cap and pressed her lips to the rim, gulping back some orangey sweetness in the hopes that it would drown all the negative feelings that were building up inside her. After finishing off the rest of the juice, Marnie stood still for a minute and evaluated her emotional state. Sure enough, nothing had changed and Marnie was miserable. However, Marnie was miserable over something else; in fact, she was upset over *someone*. Someone who she used to be very close to. Someone who cheered her on when life got ugly, but left her behind when she needed him the most.

That someone was her father.

Marnie felt her eyes welling up with tears as she pitched the empty plastic Sunny Delight bottle into the recycling bin. She couldn't believe she was upset about her parents' divorce after all this time. Usually, she just tucked these emotions away somewhere and put on a happy face until she felt better. But hiding from her sadness had been much more difficult lately, and since there was no Lizette, Dane, Sawyer, Mom, or Nola to lean on, Marnie knew she had to reach out to the only person she had left.

Marnie picked up the white cordless phone that was located on the wall in the kitchen and found her father's cell number on speed dial. As the phone rang, Marnie wondered how long it would be before her dad's number was replaced with Bald Drew Carey's digits, or some other guy down the line. Her stomach quaked at the mere thought of that.

After the sixth ring, her father's voice mail went into action.

"Hello, this is Colin Fitzpatrick. I'm unavailable right now, so please leave a message. Thanks and have a great day."

Marnie cleared her throat once the automated operator instructed her to speak at the tone.

"Hi, Dad," Marnie murmured. She couldn't think of what to say next because she had been immediately overwhelmed with memories of him — from their father-daughter four-day weekend in Montreal two years ago to all the times he'd make shadow puppets before putting Marnie to bed. Although they'd had a nice but short conversation last week, it just didn't compare to those moments they'd shared when he'd lived at home.

"Um . . . sorry to bother you. But I kind of . . . need to talk with you." Marnie's voice rattled. When she was a little girl, she had no trouble hopping on her dad's lap as he read a book, interrupting him with her problems. Everything had been simpler then.

Marnie cleared her throat again, preparing to plead with her father to call her back as soon as possible. Suddenly, the call waiting beeped and Marnie looked at the caller ID window on the phone.

It read: *Colin's cell.*

Marnie was so relieved that she began to cry. She hit the FLASH button to retrieve her father's call.

"Hi, Dad," Marnie said wearily.

"Hello, Marniebird! Sorry I just missed you." Marnie

adored the jovial yet soothing sound of her dad's NPR-talk-show-esque voice.

"That's okay. I was just leaving you a message."

Mr. Fitzpatrick paused for a second or two as though he was doing something else while talking to Marnie. "Oh, how nice. It's always great to hear from you. How've you been?"

This harmless question triggered a typhoon of anguish inside Marnie that she couldn't stop, regardless of how desperately she wanted to. Before she knew it, she was sobbing so hard, she thought she might accidentally swallow her own tonsils.

"Oh, my god, Marnie. Are you all right?" Her father's tone was definitely worried. "Tell me what's wrong."

"I *really* need to see you, Dad," Marnie managed to mumble through a bunch of sniffles. "Can you come to Poughkeepsie today?"

She sucked in a breath and held it in. Her father kept such a busy schedule and she feared that he'd say no.

"Of course, Marniebird," Mr. Fitzpatrick replied without hesitation. "I can be there in a couple hours. Just sit tight."

"Thank you," Marnie said, exhaling. "You don't know how much it means to me."

After hanging up, Marnie retreated to her father's old recliner and waited. This was one Homecoming she just couldn't afford to miss.

When Marnie wrapped her arms around her father in the doorway, it was as though she hadn't hugged him since preschool. But when she finally pulled back and gazed at him lovingly, it was like he'd never moved out of the house. Her dad still looked like Anderson Cooper — his salt-and-pepper hair was cut really short, his eyes were a sparkling shade of blue, and his kind smile radiated warmth, as usual. Just his presence alone made Marnie feel safe.

"How's my Marniebird?" her dad asked playfully.

"Better now," she replied.

"I'm glad to hear that," he said. "Your phone call worried me."

Marnie wanted to say she was sorry, but she was too busy contemplating whether or not her mom would get angry if her father came inside.

"Do you want something to eat?" her dad inquired.

Marnie grabbed her green army-style jacket and her purse off the wall rack and closed the door behind her. "Yes. Definitely."

"Great, I'm starved." Mr. Fitzpatrick fished out his

car keys from his pants pocket. "What are you in the mood for? You can have anything your pretty little heart desires."

"Well, in that case," Marnie said, linking arms with her dad, *"I scream, you scream —"*

"We all scream for ice cream!" her father finished as he unlocked Marnie's door.

"Oh, my god, we are *such* dorks," she said, giggling.

"If you ask me, your mom beats us both in the dork department." Mr. Fitzpatrick laughed and ruffled Marnie's hair.

Marnie never found these snide comments very funny, and her mom was guilty of taking cheap shots at her dad, too. However, she spent such little time with her father that bickering over the issue just wasn't worth it.

"Can we go to Stewart's?" Marnie was surprised to hear herself suggest that place. She hadn't been there since the day Nola tricked her into meeting Weston (whom, according to the list she'd found in her desk drawer, she had kissed 148 times, including yesterday's lip-lock).

"Sure," her father said. "Let's go."

Fifteen minutes later, Marnie and her dad were having a late lunch, which consisted of hot fudge cake and banana brittle sundaes. With each gooey, syrup-covered spoonful, they engaged in light small talk. Mr. Fitzpatrick told Marnie about his new apartment and his noisy upstairs neighbor. Then he went on about his job for a bit. Once her dad had scraped his ice cream dish clean, he looked Marnie right in the eyes.

"Okay, enough stalling," Mr. Fitzpatrick said. "I want to hear about what's troubling you."

Marnie shoved some ice cream into her mouth to delay the inevitable crying spell. It worked, but not for long. "Daddy, my life is a complete train wreck," she gurgled.

Her dad took her hand. "Tell me."

Without thinking about how it was going to sound or what her father might say, Marnie tearfully rehashed the first month of school, from her fisticuffs with Nola to her car wash diss-fest (minus the kiss with Weston, of course). Her dad listened carefully and didn't interrupt, which was why she always went to him with her problems.

"Wow. That was quite a story." Her father's wide-eyed expression showed just how flabbergasted he was.

Marnie blinked back tears while licking a string of caramel off her spoon. "Trust me, I wish we were talking about someone else's life."

"Well, we kind of are," her dad said.

Marnie looked at him, bewildered. "What do you mean?"

"Everything you just told me happened to the Marnie Fitzpatrick of *yesterday,*" he explained. "With each day comes the opportunity to learn from our past and yet start fresh."

"You sound like a self-help book," Marnie said, chuckling.

"I know, but that doesn't make what I'm saying any less true."

"But how can I start fresh when almost everyone *hates* me?" Marnie lowered her head and wiped her sniffling nose with a napkin.

"Marnie, the people who really matter stick with you in your toughest hour, and they don't give up on you, even when you make mistakes. When you stay true to those people, and yourself, everyone else's opinions of you won't mean a thing."

Suddenly, Marnie's mind flashed back to the day she saw Sawyer in the auditorium and what he'd said about realizing who her true friends were. Essentially her father was saying the same thing; he seemed to be encouraging her to be a better friend to herself, too.

"So I need to be a better judge of character, right?" Marnie hoped she'd understood her father's message correctly.

"Yes, but you also need to take more responsibility for your actions," her dad said. "If you had been sensitive to Nola's feelings and made her well-being a priority, she might be sitting here with us right now, just like the old days."

Marnie swallowed hard as a monsoon of Nola memories flooded the room. Her father was right — she hadn't taken good care of Nola's feelings at all. In fact, Marnie had blown Nola off whenever it came down to picking between her and Lizette. Now Marnie knew how terrible it felt to be on the flip side, but talking to her father at least helped her to see a dim light at the end of the proverbial tunnel.

"Thanks for coming to see me, Dad."

Marnie pushed her seat back so she could get up to hug her father, but she accidentally hit the chair of the person who was sitting behind her.

"Sorry about that," Marnie said sincerely.

However, the moment she realized who she was speaking to, she wished she hadn't apologized.

Jeremy "Jerk-face" Atwood: student council sparring partner and former election opponent.

"Could you *move* so I can get up?" Marnie said firmly.

"I was just leaving." Jeremy adjusted his glasses on his nose and then grabbed his messenger bag off the floor.

“Good,” Marnie said under her breath.

Jeremy left the table quickly and bolted out the door without looking back.

“Who was that?” her dad asked.

Marnie rose from her chair, walked over to her father, and gave him another hug. “It doesn’t matter, Daddy. I’m here with you.”

Sunday, October 21, 1:49 P.M.

ev=mc2: *hi nola. r u busty?*
ev=mc2: *BUSY! i meant to say BUSY*
nolaj1994: *hi evan. funny typo :0)*
ev-mc2: *embarrassing 2*
nolaj1994: *no worries. what's up?*
ev=mc2: *just wanted 2 ask a quick question about homecoming*
nolaj1994: *sure, shoot*
ev=mc2: *what color is ur dress? i want 2 get u a corsage that will match*
nolaj1994: *how nice, tx*
ev=mc2: *np, it's tradition and all*
nolaj1994: *well i haven't gotten my dress yet*
nolaj1994: *i'm going shopping with my mom this afternoon, so i guess i can call u later and let u know*
ev=mc2: *cool, hope u find something u like*
nolaj1994: *me 2, i'm not a big fan of semiformal wear*
ev=mc2: *neither am i, but u will look pretty no matter what*
nolaj1994: *sorry ev, i have 2 go now. mom is waiting . . .*
ev=mc2: *oh, ok. ttyl ☺*
nolaj1994: *bye*

Chapter 18

"So, what do you think?" Dr. James asked. Nola stood in front of a full-length mirror, draped in a pink sheet of synthetic leopard-print fabric that gathered tightly at her waist and billowed down to the floor.

"I can't wear this dress for health reasons. It's making me really sick," Nola said wryly.

Over the past three hours, Nola had gone to five different stores in the Galleria and tried on eight dresses (two in purple, four in red, and two in blue). Now she was in an extra-large fitting room at Macy's (store number six), wondering what *Project Runway* reject had designed this hideous pastel monstrosity and what girl in her right mind would wear it.

Nola was about to throw up her hands and scream, "Enough is enough!" like the diva she sometimes prayed she could be, but it was obvious her mom wasn't about to give up.

"Okay, let's have the salesperson bring us the next selection," Nola's mom said, wrapping a loose thread around her finger and tugging it free.

Nola looked away from her reflection and at her mom, who was always so well put-together when she wasn't donning ER scrubs and wearing her hair in a high bun. Today's outfit included a delicate forest-green Cole Haan wrap sweater and a charcoal-gray pencil skirt, paired with these sporty red T-strap DKNY walking shoes.

In fact, Nola thought so much of her mother's ensemble, she was considering asking for permission to wear it to the dance. That way, she'd be comfortable and classy instead of corseted and trashy. Besides, maybe then Nola could find out if Evan really meant what he said about her looking pretty no matter what (although the fact that he'd said it at all made her quite uneasy and excited).

"Mom, you know I hate clothes shopping. And I just don't like any of these frilly . . . *things*." Nola unzipped the dress in the back and let it fall to her bare feet. "I want something . . . low-maintenance."

"Low-maintenance?" Her mom made a face that showed off the one or two wrinkles on her forehead. "It's a *Homecoming* dance, Nola. Not a barn dance."

"Are you making fun of me?" Nola said. Exhaustion was definitely setting in, which meant that she was on the verge of becoming cranky.

"No," her mom said, opening the door a tad so she could keep an eye out for a fitting-room attendant. "I'm just pointing out that the objective for this afternoon was to find you the right dress for the *occasion*. And I don't think low-maintenance is what you should be going for."

Why do mothers always have to make such sense?

"Fine! But this is the *last* store. We either find something here or I'm going to the dance in my bathrobe," Nola said with a smirk.

Dr. James rubbed Nola's shoulder and smiled. "Deal. Just let me do one more lap around the floor."

Nola grinned back. "Okay. Don't forget to take the Pink Panther dress with you!"

After her mother picked up the dress and scooted out of the room, Nola fished out her phone from her bag to check and see if she had any text messages. There were two: one from Evan and one from (gulp) Matt. She opened Matt's first.

U AROUND? NEED 2 TALK 2 U. V.V. IMP.

She dialed Matt's cell right away, willing him to answer, but she was directed to his voice mail. Nola's heart sank in disappointment.

"Hey, Matt. I just got your text. Sorry I didn't call sooner but I silenced my phone because I'm out dress shopping with my mom. I'm afraid to say it's not going too well. Actually, I think Evan would be better off going to the dance with Ms. Lucas!"

Okay, Miss Boring O'Snoozerson. Stop your rambling and wrap it up!

"Anyway, I'm always here if you need me. Talk soon."

There.

Once Nola hung up, she clicked onto Evan's message and read its contents.

CAN'T WAIT 2 DANCE W U CUTIE!

What the?!

Nola's heart rate rose to jumping-jacks level. Wasn't Evan supposed to be *more* shy than she was? If so, why was he sending her flirty text messages out of the blue? Did Evan think that because Nola said she'd go with him to Homecoming, she was also agreeing to be his . . . *girlfriend*? Her warm-up date definitely hadn't prepared her for this!

Her frantic worry-mongering was interrupted by a knock on the fitting-room door. "Are you ready to see the most gorgeous dress in Poughkeepsie?" Dr. James's voice was full of enthusiasm.

"Yeah, I'm ready," Nola said numbly.

Her mother swept into the room, holding a knee-length black halter dress with elegant embroidery on the bodice. It was a lot prettier than every other dress she'd tried on, and Nola knew she should have been thrilled that her mother had found something this classy. However, all she felt was a familiar itch-itch-itch on her calf muscle.

"This is going to look fabulous on you, Nola. Put it on!"

When Nola was finished fastening the tiny buckle on the halter, she checked herself out in the mirror. She looked different than she had last night. Sure, she was wearing a fancy dress instead of her underwear, but there was something else that wasn't the same — Nola's self-perception.

She could see how long her neck was, how smooth her shoulders were, and how tiny her waist appeared. Nola was beautiful, and for the first time, she believed it. However, the moment this realization sank in, Nola thought about Evan's text and what his expectations might be and she cringed.

As soon as her mother saw Nola's frown and her reddening cheeks, she instantly jumped into Doctor Mom mode.

"Oh, honey. I thought that you'd like this one. You look so lovely in it," her mom said, affectionately running her fingers through Nola's hair.

Lovely, Nola thought. Matt had called her that just yesterday, but she felt anything but lovely right now.

"It's not that, Mom. The dress is beautiful," Nola said, her throat dry.

"Then why are you upset all of a sudden?"

This was one severely loaded question, and Nola couldn't begin to think of a way to explain how she was feeling to her mother. The pissed-off part of Nola would rather eat dirt than admit this, but the sensitive side of Nola was tired of fighting it tooth and nail. Although Nola had enjoyed spending time with her mom today, she knew that if she'd gone shopping with Marnie — just like they'd done in the old days — she would have been happy, elated even.

Nola would also have been able to confide in Marnie about her fake date with Matt, her twisted kiss with Ian, and Evan lusting after her. She would have laughed when Marnie tried to coerce Nola into taking her "stellar fashion advice" and wear a dress that showed "maximum cleave." True, Nola could have brought Iris along today for some teen-girl camaraderie, but that was the problem with stand-in friends: As good as they seem, they'll never be as good as the real thing.

"Nola? You haven't answered me."

Nola drifted out of her thoughts and back to the fitting room. She suddenly wanted to leave the Galleria as soon as possible. Maybe there was a chance she could outrun the memory of Marnie. "I'm fine, Mom. Really."

Nola's mother pouted, which indicated that she wasn't convinced. "You're not saying that like you mean it."

"I *do* mean it," Nola said, forcing a half grin. "And I think the dress is perfect. Can I have it? Please?"

"Of course you can," Dr. James said, hugging Nola from behind and putting her chin on Nola's shoulder. "God, Nola. You look so grown up. I wish your father and I weren't going to that Junior League fund-raiser next Saturday. He and I would have really loved to have seen you and Evan off."

Nola felt like groaning — if her mom and dad were going to be away, that meant Ian would be stationed at the house on the night of the dance. But instead she leaned her head against her mom's and said, "I would have loved that, too."

An hour later, Nola and her mom were weighted down with shopping bags and headed toward the Galleria exit. Nola's mom had insisted that they stop and pick up a pair of strappy black sandals at Aldo and visit Zales for some medium-size silver hoop earrings.

"I feel like we're forgetting something," Nola's mom said, examining the contents of the three bags she was holding.

"Nope, that's it. We've got everything we need. Let's go!" Nola took her free hand and grabbed her mom by the arm, dragging her toward the automated doors that were no more than fifty feet in front of them.

"Hold on, I know what we're missing." Dr. James locked her legs so that Nola couldn't pull her any farther. "Makeup! We should really go to the Chanel counter back at Macy's."

"I can just borrow some of yours, Mom. Okay? Can we go home now?" Nola implored.

"But you have your father's coloring, honey," her mom replied. "Come on. We'll only be twenty minutes."

Nola glanced up to the vaulted ceiling and silently asked the mall gods for a divine intervention.

"Carol! Carol James!" a voice called from behind them.

Slowly, Nola and her mom turned around. Standing in line at Cinnabon was a handsome man with salt-and-pepper hair, waving at them. Beside him was a girl with blonde hair and blue eyes that were dazzling, even from this distance.

"Oh, look. It's Marnie and her dad," Nola's mom said.

Nola swallowed hard. "I know."

Her mom glanced over her shoulder at Nola while waving back. "Should we go say hello, or would that be too uncomfortable for you?"

Uncomfortable wasn't quite the word Nola would use to describe how she was feeling. Actually, she wasn't sure there was an adjective in the English, Spanish, or French dictionary that could aptly express what was going on in her heart. Still, as mixed up as she was, Nola couldn't outright ignore Marnie with her mom and Mr. Fitzpatrick right there. She'd look like a first-rate jerk. And Nola hoped that Marnie would hold off on being mean to Nola under adult supervision. Perhaps this was the only way for them to talk civilly. And maybe talking civilly was just what they needed.

Nola took a deep breath and sighed warily. "Sure, Mom."

Nola's mother leaned over and whispered, "It'll be okay, Nola. Just stick close to me."

Nola smiled at her mom. Sometimes she knew exactly what to say.

As Nola approached Cinnabon, she experienced total tunnel-vision. Everything was pitch-black around her and the only person in her sights was Marnie, who looked downright dreary in a navy blue fleece and faded boyfriend-fit black jeans. It wasn't until Marnie's father gave Nola a hug that she snapped out of it.

"Wow, Nola! Look at you," Mr. Fitzpatrick said cheerily. "It's been forever since we've seen each other and you've sprouted up, what? A foot and a half?"

Nola's mom laughed. "More like a few inches, Colin. But give her another year and she'll be taller than the both of us."

Nola rolled her eyes. *Could they be any more lame?*

"And how are you doing these days, Marnie?" Nola's mother asked brightly.

Marnie chomped on her lower lip nervously. "I'm good, thanks."

But Nola knew better than to believe Marnie, especially when she looked into her ex-best friend's eyes and saw nothing but the same loneliness that Nola had been feeling since their falling-out.

"So what are you ladies doing here at the Galleria?" Mr. Fitzpatrick said as he paid the cashier for a box of Caramel Pecanbons. "We're here picking up some delicious goodies, as per Erin's demands."

Nola giggled. She'd always liked Marnie's father. He was so delightful and energetic. She never did understand why he and Mrs. Fitzpatrick couldn't get along. Then again, she never thought she'd get into a friendship-ending brawl with Marnie.

"Well, Nola and I were dress shopping," Dr. James answered.

Nola noticed how Marnie's face lit up the moment her mom had said "dress shopping." Nola's angry side begged her not to smile, but she gave in to her sensitive side.

"That's nice. What's the dress for? A wedding?"

Before Nola could respond, her mom piped up again. "Actually, Nola's going to the Homecoming dance with a very nice young man named Evan Sanders. He just won a scholarship at school. Isn't that right, Nola?"

"Um, yeah."

Nola was about to cast her eyes down at her feet, but then she caught a glimpse of a grinning Marnie. Her angry side started warming up, eager to throw fastballs at Marnie's head if she tried to mess with Nola. But her sensitive side urged Nola to be patient, and once Marnie spoke up, Nola was glad that she had listened.

"So, can I see your dress?"

Nola was almost thrown off balance by the sound of Marnie's voice. She'd somehow become used to the edginess of it, so all she could do was nod and hold the bag open for Marnie.

Marnie gently pulled out the dress and held it up in front of her, gazing at the fabric and embroidery carefully, as though it were a piece of haute couture. Nola recognized Marnie's look of approval.

"It's fantastic," Marnie said.

"Thanks." Nola blushed a little. "I just hope I don't spill something on myself and ruin it."

Marnie let out a small giggle. "Like the time you got puddle-splashed by that garbage truck when we were walking to Waryas Park? Your argyle sweater was never the same."

"Or when I leaned over that candle to give you a hug at your holiday party and set my angora scarf on fire," Nola added with a chuckle.

Marnie looked as though she was trying to squelch a laugh, but it came out loud and clear. "Oh, my god, I'll never forget that."

"Neither will I," Nola said, grinning. "I'm just glad you yelled —"

"Stop, drop, and roll!" Marnie completed Nola's thought, just like she used to.

"— or the rest of me probably would have gone up in flames." Nola's smile kept broadening as though she'd forgotten how mad she was supposed to be.

"Come on, Nola," Marnie said, her voice suddenly soft. "You know I never would have let anything like that happen to you."

Nola heaved an emotional sigh that came from deep within. Although Marnie had been the source of so much pain lately, Nola could tell that she was being sincere. "Thanks."

"Well, I guess we should get these snacks back to Erin," Mr. Fitzgerald said. He put his arm around Marnie and gave her a squeeze. When he let go, tears welled up in Marnie's eyes, but she still had a cheery smile on her face.

Honestly, Nola had never seen Marnie this fragile before. However, Marnie had never faced so many enemies before — the girl probably couldn't even count them on one hand. Nola knew that she should feel satisfied by that, but instead she felt . . . sympathy.

"It was good to see you both," Dr. James replied as she tugged Nola by the sleeve. "Take care."

"Bye, Nola," Marnie said happily. "Have a great time at the dance."

After a lukewarm good-bye, Nola waved farewell and tottered off with her shopping bags. But the farther she walked away from Marnie, the colder she felt all over.

Chapter 19

MARNIE FITZPATRICK'S
STAY POSITIVE TO-DO LIST

1) _Cosmo_ says a new shade of lipstick can change your attitude. Maybe something like shocking pink might perk me right up!
2) Download some funky R&B music to my iPod. That'll keep my spirits high during my morning runs.
3) Read something uplifting. Oprah likes that book _Eat, Pray, Love_. I'll give that a try!
4) Count my blessings right before I go to bed. I have taken so much for granted. Reminding myself of what/who really matters, like my dad said, will help me keep the right perspective.

Marnie woke up at six-thirty A.M. on Monday to do something she hadn't in over a week — take a nice long run through her neighborhood. After hitting the snooze button on her alarm twice, she slid out from under her comforter and immediately put on her New Balance cross-trainers so she wouldn't crawl back into bed. Then she threw on a pair of teal Fila jogging pants (which were a little too snug for her liking — damn those

Pecanbons!) and a lightweight long-sleeved T-shirt (a pick-me-up gift that her father had bought her at Lady Foot Locker yesterday).

While she knew that she should stretch properly before her workout, Marnie was so eager to move at a high-paced stride that she just bolted down the porch stairs and sprinted along the sidewalk. Once she reached the five-minute mark, she could feel the muscles in her leg pull a little, like they were under strain. But she carried on anyway, pumping her arms back and forth as the shock-absorption soles of her sneakers earned their keep.

When Marnie reached the first mile of her run, beads of perspiration were sliding down her forehead, neck, and collarbone. But she hadn't felt this free and alive in quite a while. It wasn't just from the endorphin rush, either. Marnie had felt pretty good yesterday after she and her father had their heart-to-heart, and even better once she'd talked with Nola at the Galleria. In fact, when Marnie had gone to sleep last night, she'd been able to drift off quickly, kind of like she had over the summer.

At one and a half miles, Marnie was in her pseudo-Zen zone — her mind was crystal clear and whatever thoughts she was having were rather optimistic and cheerful. Instead of worrying about being blacklisted from the Homecoming dance or the nightmare car wash on Saturday (not counting the kiss with Weston), she stayed focused on the simple beauty of her surroundings: the way the sky turned jelly-bean pink and orange as the sun came up over the houses; how trees with multicolored foliage lined the streets like an honor guard; the festive fall wreaths adorning front doors; the way the air whipped through her shirt, which still smelled brand-new.

All of these vivid details came together and formed an energy field around Marnie that made her feel protected and safe. And that feeling gave way to a cornucopia of Nola memories, most of them silly and happy thoughts from eighth grade, when they'd been inseparable and could finish each other's sentences. Marnie had been rather innocent and naive then, and while she'd been angry at Nola for wanting to hold on to those qualities when they started high school, lately Marnie was yearning to have them — and Nola — back.

But in order to do that, Marnie would have to forget how incredible it had been to be Lizette Levin's BFF and Dane's flavor-of-the-month, as well as swear them off for good. Even now, she wasn't convinced she could do either of those things.

Sometimes problems like these didn't get solved on morning runs.

It was almost seven-fifteen when Marnie entered the home stretch. She picked up the scent of freshly brewed hazelnut coffee coming from someone's open kitchen window. Her eyes concentrated on her badly-in-need-of-an-HGTV-guru's-magic-touch house, which, like in most rearview mirrors, was closer than it appeared. However, what stood out the most was what Marnie heard as she slowed down to a brisk walk and took her pulse. It kind of sounded like . . . footsteps. Coming from behind her. Like she was being *followed*.

Marnie gulped as her fight-or-flight response prepared to kick in. She tried to conjure up the judo move her mom had taught her (Mrs. Fitzpatrick had taken a bunch of classes after the divorce) but she was drawing a blank. That meant flight was the most logical choice in this situation. She was just about to haul ass when a speeding Sawyer Lee came flying toward her on his skateboard, shouting, "Out of my way, Marnie!"

What the HELL?!

In order to avoid a collision, Marnie dove to her right and landed face-first on Mr. and Mrs. Klein's newly mowed lawn. It took her a second to recover from the impact, but when she did, she got up and saw Sawyer leap off his skateboard and tackle a scrawny-looking boy. Actually, a scrawny-looking boy with the whitest sneakers she had ever seen.

It could only be one person: Jeremy Atwood.

Marnie dashed over to Sawyer and Jeremy, who were wrestling on the ground. Sawyer had Jeremy in some type of scissor hold and Jeremy was gripping Sawyer by the neck of his blue twill Dickies work shirt.

"Get off of me!" Jeremy yelled angrily.

"Not a chance!" Sawyer snarled.

Marnie's pulse was accelerating faster now than on her run. "Quit it, guys. You're gonna get hurt!"

"So what?" Jeremy freed his right hand somehow and jabbed Sawyer in the ribs.

"Hurt is just what this jerk needs!" Sawyer growled as he nailed Jeremy in the shoulder with his fist.

"I said *stop*!" Marnie bent over and grabbed Sawyer by the waist, pulling him off of Jeremy. "What's going on with you two?"

Sawyer panted heavily. "I saw . . . him . . . trailing you."

"No I wasn't!" Jeremy said, defiant. "Can't a guy go for a walk without getting ambushed?"

"You don't even *live* in this neighborhood," Sawyer countered. "And if you were just out for a walk, why were you aiming your *phone* at Marnie?"

"I . . . I was making a call."

Sawyer rolled his eyes. "More like taking a picture, right?"

Marnie looked down by Jeremy's leg and saw his phone lying on the pavement. She quickly reached for it, sending Jeremy into a panic. He lunged forward to stop her but Sawyer pushed him away.

Marnie flipped open the phone and went into Jeremy's images folder. There were at least a dozen unflattering photos of Marnie on her run this morning, sweating profusely and looking very haggard. There was even one of her picking a wedgie!

Oh, god, I hope we caught him before he sent these to anyone.

In a panic, Marnie whizzed through Jeremy's sent text messages, and thankfully, there were no picture messages that had been sent. However, when she looked through his in-box, she noticed that Brynne Callaway had sent Jeremy one a couple minutes ago. Marnie opened the message.

DO U HAVE PICS YET? WHAT'S TAKING SO LONG?

At last, Brynne's spy had been revealed.

"Are you going to explain yourself or what, Jeremy?!" Marnie shouted. She tossed the phone to Sawyer so the rat couldn't get to it and Sawyer could delete all the photos.

"Hey, looks like you sent some harassing texts to

Marnie just the other day," Sawyer said as he studied Jeremy's phone.

"I mean it, Atwood. Talk or I'll have Sawyer snap you in two," Marnie threatened.

"Fine! I'll talk!" Jeremy sighed and shook his head. "I just wanted to win the election, that's all."

"The election?"

"During the campaign, Brynne sent me to Stewart's to get dirt on you. She said that humiliating my opponent was the only way I could beat her," Jeremy said, his voice low. "So I heard Nola James telling Matt Heatherly that thong story, and uh . . . you know the rest."

Marnie stumbled backward as though she'd been pushed. She immediately thought back to seeing Jeremy at Stewart's when she was with her dad. How could she have not considered Jeremy a suspect? Marnie wasn't surprised that Brynne had set up this scheme, though. She knew that wench was behind it all along.

Marnie was also a bit startled to learn that Nola had told one of her most embarrassing secrets to Matt Heatherly, but then she reminded herself of how many Nola tidbits she'd leaked to the boys in her life. Anyway, if Brynne hadn't sent Jeremy out to do her dirty work, Marnie's secret probably never would have made it past the walls of Stewart's.

"Well, then why were you still spying on me afterward? The election was over and you'd lost anyway."

Jeremy's face turned turnip red. "Why do you think? I was pissed off! People voted for you because you were friends with Lizette and going out with Dane. That's totally unfair! And I actually *wanted* to be treasurer. You didn't even seem to care."

"Aren't you forgetting that *I* nominated *you*?" Marnie threw her arms up in the air.

Suddenly, Jeremy was very flustered. "Yeah, but . . . I, uh . . . it's just that—"

"I'm tired of listening to this jackass," Sawyer said. He got up off the ground and handed the phone back to Jeremy. "I deleted all the photos *and* your contacts list."

"What?!" Jeremy screeched.

"That's the least of your problems." Sawyer squatted down and looked Jeremy in the eyes. "You're going to own up to all this crap, too. Or there will be harsh consequences."

Marnie's jaw hung open. Who knew Sawyer could be this tough?!

A sheet of fear covered Jeremy's flushed face. "Okay, I'll do whatever you want. Can I go now?"

Sawyer stood up and sidled next to Marnie. "You better be outta my sight in less than ten seconds."

Holy, holy, holy crap! Sawyer is the prime minister of AWESOME!

"Ten, nine," Sawyer started to count.

Jeremy scrambled to his feet and dashed down the street with his tail between his legs. By the time Sawyer got to three, Jeremy could no longer be seen with the naked eye.

Marnie wanted to put her hand on the top of Sawyer's arm and let it slide down to his wrist, but instead she just smirked at him awkwardly. "Thank y—" she began.

"I was just in the right place at the right time," Sawyer interrupted, taking a couple steps away from Marnie. "No thanks necessary."

No thanks necessary? If Sawyer hadn't come by and tackled Jeremy, Marnie might never have known who'd been spying on her. Now she could reveal Brynne for the conniving troll she was and everyone at Poughkeepsie Central would finally embrace Marnie again. The truth was, she owed Sawyer. H-U-G-E.

"How can I ever repay you?" Once Marnie asked this question, she realized how girly it sounded.

Sawyer walked over to his skateboard, picked it up off the lawn, and put it down on the sidewalk. He hopped on and steadied himself, then gave Marnie a friendly smile, which she knew she didn't really deserve.

"I'm not sure. But when I think of something, I'll let you know."

Marnie watched Sawyer skate off and wondered what had brought him to her neck of the woods in the first place. But as she walked through the front door of her house, she got an early start on counting her blessings.

Monday, October 22, 11:35 A.M.

marniebird: *weston, can you talk?*
redsoxnumber1: *in the middle of computer lab so not 4 long*
marniebird: *i know, i'm in the library, but i need ur help*
redsoxnumber1: *u need me, eh? will i get another hot kiss? ☺*
marniebird: *do u have 2 b smug ALL THE TIME?!?!*
redsoxnumber1: *pretty much*
marniebird: *fine, forget it*
redsoxnumber1: *don't b so sensitive. What do u need help with?*
marniebird: *i kind of need*
marniebird: *a tough guy*
redsoxnumber1: *u have come 2 the right place, sexy ;-)*
marniebird: *oh puhlease, i didn't mean it like THAT*
redsoxnumber1: *2 bad 4 u*
marniebird: *ugh! why did I even bother?*
redsoxnumber1: *cuz I'm the toughest guy u know*
marniebird: *2nd toughest actually*
redsoxnumber1: *so what do u need me 2 do?*
marniebird: *meet me and sawyer lee by my locker at the end of the day and bring ur baseball bat*
redsoxnumber1: *sounds kinky*
marniebird: *it won't b when i beat u to a pulp with it!!!!!*

redsoxnumber1: *now ur talking*
marniebird: *r u going to show up or not?*
redsoxnumber1: *yes, i will*
marniebird: *okay, thx*
redsoxnumber1: *gotta go, c u later*
marniebird: *later*

Chapter 20

At three P.M. on Tuesday, Nola hunkered down in the back of the school bus. Wrapped in a thick chestnut-colored sweater coat, she sat with her knees pressed up against the olive-green seat in front of her. On her lap was her tote bag, which kept filling up with notebooks, folders, and binders as the first quarter soldiered on. Nola's classmates were chattering around her, mostly about the Homecoming dance and who was going to be crowned king or queen. The buzz was that Lizette would reign supreme on Saturday, but Nola found herself hoping that a certain underdog would win.

As Nola waited for the bus to depart, she thought about how strange it was that after her brief encounter with Marnie on Sunday, the angry side of her that wanted to clobber her ex-friend and anyone else who dared step to her, had been quite subdued. Nola wasn't a fool, though. She wasn't about to push all that happened between them under the rug just because they'd been nice to each other for a few minutes. However, it did feel good — if not liberating — to release some of that animosity toward Marnie.

But Nola had definitely seen a glimmer of her old friend at the Galleria, and maybe, just maybe there was a chance they could make up. Nola had one condition: Marnie would have to apologize and take responsibility for her actions. Otherwise, how could Nola ever truly trust or count on her again?

"Mind if I bum a ride?"

Nola glanced up and saw Matt's head peeking out from the seat in front of her, his beautiful hazel eyes very red again.

"I think that's a question for the bus driver," she replied, smirking.

"Well, he's currently bumming cigarettes off Sawyer, so I figured he wouldn't mind. 'Cuz if he did, he'd be a hypocrite and nobody likes that quality in a public servant," Matt said, pushing unruly strands of hair away from his forehead with his calloused fingertips.

Nola laughed, just as hard as she had on their warm-up date. It hadn't been easy to keep her cool since she'd left that voice-mail message on Sunday. Matt never returned her phone call and he hadn't been in school yesterday. As for today, he arrived at PoCen just after their physics class started, so they hadn't had an opportunity to catch up. However, once Matt slid into the seat next to her, she could tell that whatever had been V.V. IMP on Sunday wasn't good. He was wringing his hands and his shoulders were hunched forward.

“Sorry I didn’t call you back the other day. Things have been . . .” Matt trailed off for a second before sighing sadly. “Rather insane.”

Nola reached over and rubbed her hand lightly on Matt’s back. She loved the soft feel of his cotton long-sleeve tee. “What’s wrong?”

“Everything,” Matt said, sniffing. “My dad and I went to Binghamton on Sunday. The police got an anonymous tip about my mom and they’re following a really strong lead right now.”

Nola’s mouth fell open. “Wow. But that’s good news, right?”

“I don’t know. They told us not to get too excited. Sometimes the tips go nowhere.” Matt rolled his head and loosened his neck muscles. “It’s just that . . . there’s more.”

“Okay.” Nola stopped rubbing Matt’s back and gripped her heavy tote bag with two clammy hands.

“There’s something you have to understand, Nol.” Matt’s voice was gritty. “For a long time, my father thought that my mother had walked out on us. They’d been arguing a lot and she’d threatened to leave before.”

Nola listened quietly, hoping that whatever Matt was about to tell her wouldn’t hurt too badly.

“But I never believed that. *Never*.”

"Why not?"

"Because she may have wanted to get away from my dad, but she didn't want to get away from me."

Nola could understand that sentiment more than Matt would ever know.

"She loved me, Nol. Not that my dad doesn't, but if my mom wanted to walk out on him, she would have taken me with her," Matt said in a near whisper.

"I think you're right," Nola said.

Matt's hands were now balled into fists. "Well, now my dad *finally* sees the light. And . . . uh . . . he wants to be . . . um . . . closer to the investigation."

There was a very long, silent pause that Nola had no desire to break. She knew what Matt would say next. Not only was it going to hurt but it was going to feel as though someone had driven a railroad spike into her aorta.

"So we're moving to Binghamton for a while."

Make that two railroad spikes.

Nola clutched her bag tightly, praying that would somehow keep her from blubbering. "How long is a while?"

"I guess until she's found." Matt gazed into Nola's eyes, which were already watery. "Are you upset?"

Nola let out a small giggle. "Me? Upset? What makes you think that?"

Matt glanced out the window as the bus finally pulled away from the curb. "It'll be okay, Nola. I promise."

Nola's chest tightened, indicating that nothing would be okay once Matt left Poughkeepsie.

"When do you leave?" Nola muttered.

"On Friday."

"*Friday?*" Nola hadn't seen that coming. Friday was three days from now. How was she going to come to terms with being *separated indefinitely* from her *soul mate* in THREE DAYS?!

"Yeah. I've known about this for a while. Since before you came over to my house when the story broke, actually."

The Home Depot trip. All those cardboard boxes. Oh, my god.

"But why didn't you say anything?" Nola felt a hot tear wiggle its way down her cheek. Matt brushed it away with his thumb.

"Isn't it obvious?" He smiled. "I didn't want to ruin all our regularly scheduled fun. Or our date."

Nola thought back to Saturday night and remembered how Matt had taken her to a rooftop, just so he could make her smile as the full moon cast light all around them.

"So this means you're not going to the Homecoming dance," Nola managed.

Matt sighed. "I'm afraid not. And Riley was definitely not happy."

Who freaking cares about Riley?!

"Well, it's not your fault you can't make it," Nola said, trying to show him her support even though she wanted him to be at the dance more than anything.

"Tell that to her. And she's really wigging out about me moving farther away from her. It's like she thinks I'm doing this to piss her off or something." Matt took a fist and drove it into the seat hard. "I just wish that she was more understanding. I wish she was more like . . . you."

Who knew there was room for a third spike?

Nola covered her warm face with her hands so Matt couldn't see her cry. But it didn't matter really, because when Matt put his arms around Nola and held her close, she could feel a sprinkle of salty tears wetting the roots of her long brown hair.

Once Nola got home from school, she dumped her book bag on the living room floor, stretched out on the window seat, and tried to distract herself with some jewelry-making therapy. After stringing three crystal copper beads onto a strand of thin red silk thread, Nola stopped cold and stared at her trembling hands.

Matt was moving away — *her* Matt.

Nola wiped her runny nose with the back of her

hand and attempted to concentrate on her project. She knew that if she didn't keep busy, she'd just hide out in her bedroom and cry for hours. However, a phone call interrupted Nola as she rolled the seventh bead between her fingers.

Nola set her materials on the side, reached for her bag, and pulled out her phone. When she looked at the caller ID, Nola groaned as though a telemarketer was on the other end.

EVAN.

Nola felt bad for not wanting to pick up, but this was the *fifth* time Evan had called in the last two days. The first two calls were about coordinating their outfits — apparently Evan wanted his tie and socks to match Nola's accessories somehow. The next call was about her food preference. The fourth was about her medical history — he wanted to make sure she wasn't allergic to anything or had any ocular disabilities (probably a hint about the laser-light show).

Since Nola was feeling like such a head case, she silenced her phone and waited for him to leave a message. After her cell's voice-mail indicator beeped, Nola typed in her password and listened.

"Hey, Nola. It's Evan. I just got a confirmation call from Platinum Coach and they'd like to know if we want a black or white stretch limo. Personally, I think classic black is nicer but if

you prefer white, I'll make that happen. Give me a ring as soon as you get this message, okay? Bye."

Nola's mouth went slack as she hung up the phone.

Stretch limo? Evan had never mentioned a limo of *any* kind before this! True, lots of kids took limousines to semiformals, and since neither of them could drive, it kind of made sense. Still, Nola couldn't disregard the happy lilt in Evan's voice or how eager he was to impress her. It was sweet and flattering and everything, but Nola knew just how disappointed Evan was going to be when he realized the feeling wasn't mutual.

"Can I talk with you for a bit?"

Nola looked up from her lap and saw Ian, standing next to the window with his hands behind his back.

"I really wish you'd stop sneaking up on me," she said in a clipped tone.

"Well, I saw you were on the phone and I didn't want to bother you," Ian said defensively.

Nola gazed into Ian's stormy eyes and let some of her tension fall away. "Look, I didn't mean to —"

"No, it's okay. You have every right to be annoyed with me. I was a total schmuck on Saturday." Ian tilted his head to the side and frowned.

"What are you talking about? You're *always* a schmuck," Nola joked. She'd just remembered that Ian had seen her in her underwear and hoped that he would laugh instead of notice how much she was blushing.

Ian chuckled, but only a little. "I'm being serious, Nola. In fact, I sent the boys to play in the backyard so we could be alone for a bit."

Nola swallowed hard. Ian wanted to be *alone* with her?

Ian saw Nola's tense reaction and immediately clarified. "So we can *talk*. About . . . that night in your room."

Now Nola was even more tense! "Oh, okay," she mumbled.

"Not that you have to say much." Ian ran both his hands through his hair and sighed in frustration. "It was all my fault."

Up until now, Nola had wondered what was going on in Ian's mind when he'd kissed her, and here was her chance to ask. But for some reason, she stayed quiet.

Ian shifted around uncomfortably, like he wanted Nola to speak up. When she didn't, he cleared his throat.

"Anyway, it was a stupid thing for me to do. And wrong. *Very* wrong. I just wanted to apologize and admit that I shouldn't have done it. Or even *thought* about doing it, really. Because it was stupid. With a capital S.

Actually, you can capitalize the whole word, that's how stupid it was. And it won't happen again, I swear. So yeah. That about covers it. Unless you want to see me grovel."

Nola knew she was supposed to take Ian's act of contrition seriously, but his rambling, nervous speech was so *un*-Ian-like that she laughed. "I think you already did."

Ian grinned and relaxed a little. "Can you believe I practiced that for days?"

"No, not really."

"Well, I hope I'm forgiven," Ian said wistfully.

Nola didn't quite know how to respond. She had never been mad at Ian for kissing her — just confused. Still, she knew Ian was right. Even though it felt *amazing* to kiss him, they shouldn't be messing around. Besides, easing his mind with an "apology accepted" would certainly clear the tension between them.

"Yes, I forgive you," Nola said with a smile.

"Thanks." When Ian smiled back, Nola tried not to think about how soft his lips looked. "We'll just keep it businesslike from now on."

Nola furrowed her brow. "Businesslike?"

"Right, the hired help shouldn't fraternize with the boss's little girl," Ian said, still smiling.

Now Nola was trying not to think of how she wanted to deck Ian in the chin. *"Fraternize? Little girl?!"*

Ian's smile vanished. "What?"

Nola stood up and put her hands on her hips. "If you're going to patronize me, then I take back my forgiveness."

"I *wasn't* patronizing you," Ian snapped.

Nola sneered. "Was too."

"God, this is what I mean! You are such *a child,*" Ian said, extremely perturbed.

Nola was just about to fling an insult in Ian's obnoxious (yet gorgeous) face when he backed away, completely stunned, and scrambled out of the room.

Perhaps it was something she said.

Chapter 21

At the start of Wednesday afternoon's student council meeting, Marnie had requested that she and Jeremy Atwood have the floor for a few minutes after new business was conducted. Fifteen minutes later, Marnie rose from her seat in the front row of lecture hall four and approached the podium with her head held high. In a black-and-white polka-dot shirt and a fitted cropped red jacket, Marnie knew she looked flawless. She'd spent hours this morning making sure that every strand of her blonde hair was in place and her outfit was unmistakably . . . boss. On days of vindication like this one, who could settle for anything less?

As she wet her lips and prepared to talk into the microphone, Marnie glanced toward the back row and stared at the Gap-toothed Demon, who was sitting listlessly next to Andrew Leshinsky and Lizette. While it was obvious that Brynne planned to whisper her way through Marnie's speech, Marnie smiled inside, knowing that once she introduced Jeremy, she'd have everyone's full attention. Even Dane might tear himself away from his side conversation with Weston, who winked at Marnie the moment she cleared her throat and said, "My fellow Hawks."

Just like Marnie suspected, Brynne sneered at her and elbowed Lizette in the ribs. Lizette rolled her eyes and zipped her pale green fur-hooded puffer vest, all the way up to her chin. Then Brynne had the audacity to plug her ears with her fingers and mouth, "Bite me."

But instead of getting frazzled, Marnie brought her shoulders back so that she stood as tall as a giraffe, channeled her chi at the center of her body, and continued on.

"As most of you know, when I was campaigning for freshman class treasurer, my posters were vandalized." Marnie paused for a second and looked at Dane, who was stifling an obnoxious yawn. A couple of weeks ago, he had asked her to go to the Homecoming dance. A couple of weeks before that, he was playing kissing games with her in the AV room and counting the reasons why he thought she was pretty. Now that Marnie was staring down a moment of truth, she was having trouble remembering what she had actually liked about Dane.

Not like that was a bad thing.

"The person who committed this crime was never found. However, I am pleased to announce that a classmate of ours has come forward to confess, not only to this act of wrongdoing but to others as well."

Marnie heard a door squeak open in the back of the lecture hall and saw that Principal Baxter had arrived, right on time. Marnie and the very intimidating duo of Sawyer and Weston (who'd brought his baseball bat along) had escorted Jeremy to Principal Baxter's office after school on Monday. There, they all had decided that it would be in everyone's best interest if Jeremy waited to make his public admission of guilt at the scheduled student council meeting today. It was part of his punishment, along with two weeks of restricted lunch periods and study halls. As for Brynne, only Principal Baxter knew what was in store for her.

As soon as everyone in the room saw the highest-ranking Poughkeepsie Central official standing with his arms crossed in front of his chest, there was a low hum of chatter in the room that sounded like an electric transformer. Marnie watched happily as Brynne chewed on her fingernails and Lizette's eyes widened with interest. Marnie had a very strong feeling that when all was said and done, Lizette would definitely stop being so hostile toward her. But could Marnie and Lizette go back to the way things were?

"I ask that Jeremy Atwood approach the podium, please, and address the group," Marnie said as she raised her hand and beckoned her classmate.

The crowd gasped collectively as a dejected and humiliated Jeremy trudged up to the center of the room. Once Marnie stepped back and gave Jeremy some space near the podium, he wiped at his pink eyes and then straightened his blue tie. For a brief moment, Marnie kind of felt sorry for Jeremy. Although he was a sore loser and a total pest, she had a strong feeling that Jeremy wouldn't have behaved so rashly if Brynne hadn't gotten her disgusting hooks into him. Marnie snapped her gaze back up to Brynne again, who was looking upon the scene in pure horror.

How's this for karma, scum-sucker?

Jeremy opened a folded sheet of paper and inhaled deeply before piping up. "I'm here today to offer my apologies to Marnie Fitzpatrick for sabotaging not only her campaign but her personal life as well."

Another audible gasp came from the student council members and their constituents while Weston gave Marnie a thumbs-up.

Oh, it gets better.

"In addition to ruining her posters, I have also" — Jeremy blotted his forehead with the palm of his hand — "followed her and made up stories about her. These lies have really hurt Marnie's feelings and for that I am sorry."

Marnie nodded and sighed in relief. Regardless of whether or not Jeremy's apology was sincere (and it did sound that way), soon this nightmare she'd been living would be over!

"Nothing that you've heard about Marnie and Sawyer Lee is true," Jeremy said, keeping his eyes focused on his paper.

Marnie once again glanced at Lizette, whose jaw was currently on the floor. As for Brynne, she was already starting to cry.

"And nothing I can say will be able to undo what I've done." Jeremy paused and looked up at Brynne and her melting mascara. "But I can start telling the truth now. The truth is, I didn't do any of this alone, and you have a right to know the identity of my partner."

Wait for it . . . wait for it.

"Brynne Callaway," Jeremy said unflinchingly.

If Marnie had a dollar for every "Oh, my god!" that was uttered after Jeremy implicated Brynne, she'd have enough for a brand-new wardrobe.

Principal Baxter walked down the center aisle and stopped at the row where Brynne was sitting. "Miss Callaway, come with me," he said with a menacing stare.

Brynne sniffled and wiped at her eyes, accidentally smearing black makeup onto her cheeks. She glanced at

Lizette for some type of approval, but Lizette just sat there in shock. Then Brynne turned her gaze to Marnie, who just waved at her and mouthed, "Later, loser."

"Let's go, young lady," Principal Baxter barked impatiently.

Brynne got up from her seat, shimmied her skirt down so it barely touched the top of her knees, and followed Principal Baxter out the door — guilty as charged.

Student council ended the meeting early on account of nobody being able to cease talking about the juiciest piece of gossip since the last false rumor that went around about Marnie.

Marnie spent the next few minutes talking with people who had ignored her for more than a week — Sally Applebaum and her crew, along with senior Majors Deirdre and Kerri-Anne. Many of them were saying how awful Brynne was and how much they admired Marnie for the gracious way she'd handled herself. It made Marnie feel really strong, like she could stand up for what she believed in and gain the respect of the people who mattered, exactly like her father had said.

Only the one person who really did matter hadn't come to speak with her yet. Marnie searched the crowd for Lizette when the room had emptied out somewhat, but she was nowhere to be found. Marnie's heart sank a little. Eventually, Dane slipped out, and so did Weston, and soon Marnie was left in the lecture hall alone. She'd hoped that Lizette would have at least stayed so that —

Suddenly, there was a tap on her shoulder.

Marnie spun around and saw Lizette right behind her, perched on two-inch wooden heels.

"Hey, Zee," Marnie said cheerily, just like she used to when Lizette snuck up on her.

But Lizette didn't appear cheery at all. Actually, from the way her face was scrunched up into a mass of weird and unflattering wrinkles, Marnie thought she seemed pretty damn mad.

"How could you?" Lizette spat out.

Marnie was flabbergasted. "How could I what?"

A vein in Lizette's neck was going haywire. "Obliterate Brynne like that in front of *everyone*!"

Marnie almost ripped chunks of hair out of her head. Did Lizette's brain go on a trip through the cosmos while Jeremy was telling everyone how Brynne had obliterated *Marnie*?

"Zee, I've been trying to tell you that Brynne has had it in for me since day one," Marnie replied. "Now there's proof, and you still don't believe me?!"

"That's not the point." Lizette cracked her gum loudly for emphasis.

"Then what is?" Marnie said, her voice loaded with frustration.

"You should have brought Jeremy to *me* first. And then I could have straightened everything out through word of mouth."

"Oh yeah. Like how you straightened everything out when you thought I was messing around with Sawyer?"

"Exactly. Anyway, I still think you have a thing for him. Don't deny it," Lizette said.

Marnie wanted to take Lizette's bait and tell her that Sawyer was the only guy on Marnie's Ultimate Crush of All Time list. But she knew that would only inflame the situation, so she forced Lizette to stay on the subject.

"Zee, I shouldn't have to defend what I did. Brynne and Jeremy were spreading vicious lies about me. You should be outraged like everyone else!"

"*Don't* tell me what to do, Marnie," Lizette said, narrowing her eyes and angrily snapping her fingers in front of Marnie's face. "And *don't* call me Zee. Only my *friends* can use that nickname, remember?"

Marnie was awestruck. In the time it took Lizette to snap her fingers, Marnie finally saw her for who she really was — a cold-hearted, mean-spirited, and manipulative girl . . . with the power to squash Marnie and her rising reputation like a bug.

Even so, Marnie couldn't buckle under the pressure. Not now, when she'd earned her moment in the righteous spotlight.

"You know what, *Lizette*?" Marnie said, squaring her shoulders so she felt very tall and strong. "I don't think you have *any freaking idea* of what real friendship is about."

With that, Marnie strode proudly past the Almighty Lizette Levin and out of the lecture hall doors.

Chapter 22

Nola was relieved that Hoe Bowl wasn't too busy on Thursday night. This way, only a handful of people could witness the saddest display of athleticism Poughkeepsie had ever seen. She'd had bad games before — including the time she and Marnie had bowled a combined score of 76. However, never in her life had she rolled five gutter balls in a row. Any second now, Nola's teammate would chew her out mercilessly. After all, a lot was at stake. It was Girls vs. Boys at Matt's going-away party, and Iris had made a hefty wager based on Nola's status as a Hoe Bowl regular.

As Nola returned to the seating area, her rented sky-blue bowling shoes gliding along the freshly waxed floor, she counted down in her head.

Five, four, three, two . . .

"Is your arm broken or is your inability to hit a single pin strictly neurological?" Iris said bitingly as she tallied up another goose egg for Nola on the electronic scoreboard.

Nola stuffed her hands into her jeans pockets and plopped down on an orange plastic chair. She knew exactly why she was playing like crap, but what was the point of admitting to everyone that she was hopelessly in love with Matt? He was leaving tomorrow and had no idea when he'd be coming back. The chances of anything happening between them were sub-nil, if such a term existed.

"Well, at least Nola can keep the ball *in her own lane*." Matt was waving one of his hands over the air vent on the ball-return machine, looking unbelievably scrumptious in a cranberry waffle-knit shirt and his favorite pair of worn-in jeans. "Where did you learn how to bowl, Iris? The Shot-put Academy?"

Nola let out a belly laugh, but composed herself when she saw Iris narrow her eyes and mutter something under her breath. Then Nola counted down in her head again. This time she was waiting for the all-encompassing sadness to kick in when she allowed herself to contemplate what life would be like without Matt's jokes and wit and creativity and sweetness and every other quality she adored.

Five, four, three, two . . .

"Maybe you just need some caffeine, Nol. Or some imitation-cheese-covered nachos," Evan said excitedly, polishing his bowling ball with a clean white rag. "That might help spike your energy!"

Although his good friend was moving miles away, Evan was in Mary Poppins–like high spirits, and Nola could guess why. Homecoming was two days away, and while Nola knew she should be thrilled that a kind, cute boy like Evan had been grinning at her across the lane all night long, she just felt uncomfortable.

"Yeah, well, I'm all for force-feeding Nola if that will stop her from sucking." Iris grabbed her Hollister rag bag and got up from her chair. "I'm calling a time-out for a snack bar run."

"I'll go with you. Nola's snacks are on me," Evan said with a wink. He put his ball on a rack and straightened his old-school *Price Is Right* T-shirt.

"Hey, Ev! This is *my* bon voyage party. Shouldn't you be treating *me*?" Matt said, pretending to be offended.

Evan put his hand on Matt's shoulder and gave him a sympathetic look. "Sorry, man. Nola's *way* prettier than you are."

Nola tilted her head down so she couldn't make eye contact with either of them. Not because she was embarrassed, though. Oddly enough, Nola kind of liked the fact that Evan had just complimented her in front of Matt. It made her feel very . . . *desired*. Nola had a secret hope that Evan's attention might prompt Matt to make a bold move. Or *any* move, for that matter.

"Ugh, will you stop drooling over your Homecoming date long enough to help me get the eats?" Iris huffed, tapping her red bowling shoe on the ground impatiently. "Chop-chop, Sanders!"

Nola glanced up in time to see Evan roll his warm brown eyes. Then he galloped over to Iris and they walked toward the snack bar, leaving Nola and Matt to listen to the frequent cursing of a rowdy group of overweight truckers, who occupied the next lane.

Matt placed one hand on his hip and scratched the back of his neck with the other. "Okay, Evan has officially moved out of Shy City and settled in Suaveville. What a break for you, right?"

Nola shrugged. She really didn't want to talk about Evan right now.

"Can I ask you a question?" Matt's eyebrows rose curiously.

Nola gulped hard, wondering if she and Matt would ever be alone together like this again. "Sure."

"Why are you being such a fun anchor?"

Nola laughed out loud. "A *fun anchor*?"

"Yeah, your moping is really bringing me down," Matt said.

Nola fidgeted with a loose piece of thread on the bottom of her off-white tunic sweater. "Sorry, I didn't mean to ruin the party. I guess I'm just . . ." Nola's voice trailed off.

"You didn't ruin anything." Matt sat beside Nola and folded his hands in his lap. "But this is my last night here and I don't want my most recent memories of you to be all gloom and doom."

"I know, I'll put on a happy face," Nola said with a half grin.

"No, that's not what I meant." Matt leaned back and put his arm around her. "I don't want you to *pretend* to be in a good mood. I actually want you to *be* in a good mood."

Nola's half grin disappeared. Why was Matt saying this? Didn't he know how painful this situation was for her? Of course, she wanted Matt to find some sort of peaceful resolution when it came to his mother, but she also wanted him to *stay in Poughkeepsie*!

"Listen, just because I'm leaving town for a while doesn't mean we have to get all weepy and reenact that gut-wrenching farewell scene we had on the bus. I'm not dying, I'm just relocating to a new zip code," Matt went on. "We'll talk on the phone. We'll e-mail. I might even send you a postcard or two. How does that sound?"

It sounds utterly horrible, Nola thought. But like many times before, Matt's cell phone interrupted her right when she was about to speak her mind.

"Hold on, Nol. Let me take this real quick," Matt said, scrambling to find his cell in his front pocket.

Nola nodded and yanked on the sweater thread hard so it tore off.

Matt flipped his phone open once he took a peek at the number. "Hey, Rye. What's up?"

Nola felt as though Matt had dropped his bowling ball on her foot.

"I'm at my going-away party," Matt said as he got up and wandered underneath the scoreboard. "With Iris and Evan and . . . um . . . Nola."

Was it Nola's imagination or did Matt's voice crack a little when he said her name?

Matt paced back and forth anxiously for a minute before speaking up again. "You're being ridiculous, you know that? We've gone over this a zillion times."

Nola's pulse quickened. It definitely seemed from Matt's strained tone that he and Riley were in some sort of fight.

"I'm not going to stop hanging out with her because you tell me to, okay?" Matt's cheeks flushed. "She's my friend, that's why!"

Oh, my god. Matt and Riley are fighting over ME? I CAN'T FREAKING BELIEVE THIS!

When Nola and Riley had hung out at Deirdre Boyd's party a couple weeks ago, she didn't think Riley had one insecure bone in her body. But apparently she did feel threatened by Nola. Maybe Riley was afraid that

Nola's secret wishes about Matt had a chance of coming true.

"Don't do this, Riley. Don't —" Matt took the phone away from his ear (obviously he'd been hung up on), closed it, and returned it to his front pocket. Then he just stood there, staring out at the ten bowling pins at the end of their lane, looking as though he wanted to knock them all down with his fists.

Nola got up slowly, walked over to Matt, and stood beside him. Together, they gazed out into space silently while the overweight truckers high-fived and guzzled beer out of purple plastic cups. Then out of the blue, Matt said something that Nola had longed to hear since the day she'd first visited him at his house.

"I think Riley and I just broke up."

As Nola's heart did a hundred cartwheels, she thought about running over to the truckers and pouring beer over their heads in celebration. However, when she looked at Matt's amazing profile, she could see that he appeared a bit somber. She had to settle down and act sympathetic, or at least concerned.

"Are you okay?" Nola asked as she put her hand on Matt's lower back. She closed her eyes for a second and willed herself not to think about how close her fingers were to his perfect butt.

"I'll be fine." Matt took a deep breath, turned to

Nola, and smiled. "Let me give you some unsolicited advice, Nol."

"All right."

"Stay away from possessive chicks in cool girls' clothing. You'll regret it if you don't," Matt said, pulling off his blue rubber RF FOREVER BRACELET and flinging it bow-and-arrow style toward the jolly truckers. Unfortunately the bracelet only landed a few inches away.

Nola and Matt both laughed.

"That thing's sorry excuse for a maiden flight is kind of symbolic of the relationship. Only able to go a short distance," he said, smirking.

Nola was about to agree but before she could chime in, the lights at Hoe Bowl suddenly dimmed and the disco balls that hung above each lane starting spinning around, beaming lively shades of color everywhere. Then a voice came over the loudspeaker.

"Matthew 'Stud-weiser' Heatherly. Your friends say that this is your last night in Poughkeepsie. We folks at the Hoe want to wish you the best and there's no better way to do that than *wiiiiiiith . . . Boogie Bowl!*"

"He didn't just say "Boogie Bowl," did he?" Matt said, laughing hysterically.

The microphone cut out with a screech and the seventies classic "Shake Your Booty" echoed throughout the bowling alley. By the start of the first verse, the truckers were twirling around in their lane like go-go dancers.

"You know, I don't think I'll have to pretend to be in a good mood after this," Nola said, giggling.

"Awesome." Matt grabbed Nola's hand and started disco dancing. "Come on now. You gotta boogie-oogie-oogie!"

Nola grinned and moved to the beat with Matt, totally unaware that Iris and Evan had just come back with piles of junk food. But soon they joined Nola and Matt in the lane, performing goofy dance moves and mimicking one another like silly little kids. It was almost as though Matt wasn't U-Hauling off to Binghamton in less than twenty-four hours. In fact, Nola had somehow fooled herself into thinking that tomorrow would be just another day, yet filled with even more opportunity now that Riley Finnegan was out of the picture.

Chapter 23

REASONS WHY THE HOMECOMING DANCE
IS FOR LOSERS

So much for the perk-me-up list. Looks like I'm the big loser. Sigh.

While taking Brynne Callaway down like a seasoned prizefighter had given Marnie a substantial amount of joy (Brynne ended up with a one-day, in-school suspension — ouch), it still hadn't changed the fact that Marnie's Friday night would consist of the following: digging into the Halloween candy that her mom had bought, reading a selection of high-brow fashion magazines like *Vogue* and *Elle*, and sloughing the dry skin off her heels. Everyone else Marnie knew had other plans, though. It was Homecoming eve, of course, and Majors, Minors, Wannabes, Leeks, and all those in between would be on the party circuit after the football game between the Poughkeepsie Central Hawks and the Iona Prep Gaels.

Not that Marnie cared. The truth had been out there for two days now, and while Lizette didn't seem to give the slightest crap about Marnie's innocence or their friendship, Marnie had salvaged her integrity from the clutches of a gap-toothed gossip-monger. That was reward enough, right? She didn't need to be reunited with Lizette and the rest of her disciples. She didn't need the adoration of the masses, either. Marnie was sprawled on her bed, surrounded by Hershey's Miniatures, Anna Wintour, and Burt's Bees Coconut Foot Crème! What more could a girl ask for?

How about a date to the Homecoming dance and one friend who actually cares about me? Marnie thought as she popped a tiny Mr. Goodbar into her mouth.

It was as if her sister could smell Marnie's vulnerability from across the hall. Without so much as a knock on the door, Erin flew into Marnie's room dressed like a poor man's version of Nikki Hilton and stood in front of Marnie's bed as though she was about to swat her little sister.

"Oh, god, what did I do wrong now?" Marnie said, throwing her hands up in surrender.

Somehow Erin's ocean-blue eyes turned demon-red. "Why aren't you getting ready?"

Marnie stared at Erin, baffled. "Ready for what?"

"For Lizette's tailgating party. It starts at six, so" — Erin lunged forward and grabbed Marnie by the arms — "get off your ass!" Erin yanked hard, sending Marnie to her feet.

"Let go of me, you airhead!" Marnie wriggled out of

Erin's grasp and retreated to the other side of the room. "I have no idea what you're talking about."

"What do you mean? I ran into Lizette on campus this afternoon and she told me to bring you tonight," Erin said, exasperated.

Marnie shook her head in awe. After the way Lizette had treated her on Wednesday, she had the nerve to send her older sister as a peacekeeping messenger? Why was Lizette reaching out now? And why didn't she just ask Marnie to come to the tailgating party herself instead of using Erin as a go-between? It all seemed very . . . suspicious.

"Well, I . . . I don't feel like going, okay? Anyway, what if Brynne is there? I'm sure she and her minions are waiting to eat me alive and then regurgitate me on the back lawn." Marnie fell backward onto her bed and stared up at the ceiling.

Then she noticed how silent the room was. Erin wasn't bitching and moaning. Or talking at all, for that matter. Something was dreadfully wrong. Marnie leaned up on her arms a bit so she could get a look at her sister, and what she saw surprised her.

Erin was . . . pensive. As in thinking quietly to herself before she blurted out something mean and insensitive.

Wooooooooow.

"So let me get this straight." Erin made herself comfortable on Marnie's swiveling desk chair and looked Marnie right in the eyes. "You're not going to this party because you're afraid of Brynne?"

Marnie sat up the rest of the way. "I'm *not* afraid of her. I just . . . don't want . . . okay, maybe I am a little afraid. Can you blame me?"

"No, I can't. That girl needs a full-blown colonic to flush out the bug that crawled up her butt," Erin said, laughing at her own joke. "Still, you got her good the other day. I heard a lot of buzz from both past and present Majors. They were really impressed by what you did."

A satisfied smile flashed across Marnie's face. "Really?"

"I don't say nice things very often. Don't make me repeat them," Erin said.

"Fine. But I don't see why it matters. Zee was pissed that I hosed Brynne off in public and she hasn't said a word to me since then."

"So what? Maybe she has come around and told Brynne to cash out her chips," Erin suggested. "You won't find out unless you go."

Marnie sat still for a moment and contemplated her options. She could very well attend this party with her sister and pray that it wasn't a well-laid trap of Brynne's.

She could show up and find out that Lizette really did want to make amends. Or she could stay home and avoid all of the stress that went along with being friends with the Majors.

It was strange. A week ago, Marnie would have killed to have been penciled back into Lizette's social calendar, but as she took stock of her feelings, she realized that being out of the loop had given her some perspective. Being Lizette's friend was *work*. Hard work. While Marnie had thought the effort was worth it — and it *really* was in the boy, clothes, and party departments — she didn't think putting herself through the fire pit of popularity would be any less dangerous the second time around. There were going to be more minefields and more enemies disguised as friends. (Kind of like Sawyer suggested at Alicia Blair's party.)

There was a time when Marnie didn't have to worry about any of that. She had someone who was loyal to her and would stand by her in any situation, good or bad. She had a person to confide in, to worry with, and to tell dark thoughts to. She never had to second-guess this friend, who showed Marnie over and over the depths of her devotion.

But that bridge had been burned, if not completely napalmed. More and more, Marnie was feeling the true extent of her regret, right down to her bones. When she thought about what she had given up and compared it to what she had now, the regret grew even deeper.

"Have fun at the party, Erin. I'm going to sit this one out," Marnie said, her tone soft. She wanted Erin to leave her room so she could bury her head under her Martha Stewart pillow and cry.

"What about the Homecoming dance? Are you going to sit out on *that*, too?" Erin jumped off Marnie's chair and thrust her hands on her hips.

"Well, gee, I don't have *anyone* to go with, so *yes*, I'm skipping it," Marnie barked, figuring if she raised the volume of her voice, Erin would get the point a lot quicker.

"If I can get you nominated to the Homecoming court after the inauguration party fiasco, I can certainly get you a date," Erin said arrogantly.

Marnie rolled her eyes as her sadness gave way to furiousness. "I don't want to go to the dance with some dufus of yours, so *forget it*."

"Ugh, you are insufferable, Marnie!" Erin said with sheer frustration. "Can't you see that I'm trying to *help* you?"

Marnie let out a bellowing, sarcastic laugh that could probably be heard from their dad's apartment in Connecticut. "You only help me when you're trying to help *yourself*. So what's in it for you, huh? I can't wait to hear it!"

Erin swallowed hard twice before she stormed over to the door, her eyes glistening. "There wasn't anything in it for me this time, Marnie. I was just . . . just —"

"What? What!" Marnie shouted. She was so upset right now that she wanted to kick something with all her might.

"I was just trying to be your friend for a change," Erin said as a tear spilled down her right cheek.

At first, Marnie flinched. She hadn't expected something that heartfelt to come out of her sister's mouth. Then she felt a few prickles of guilt. Although Erin didn't act like she had feelings, she certainly possessed them. Marnie regretted being so cross.

"Erin, wait. I'm sor —"

"You know what, Marnie? It always sucked knowing you'd rather have Nola as your sister than me," Erin snapped, and shut the door behind her.

Marnie rubbed her cheek as though Erin had just slapped it. True, Marnie had always preferred hanging out with Nola to being with Erin. But what hurt Marnie the most was the realization that she had read Erin's intentions completely wrong, just like she had with her so-called friends and boyfriends countless times before.

What terrified Marnie to the core was the fear that she would never get it right.

Friday, October 26, 10:52 P.M.

redsoxnumber1: *hey buddy ;-)*
marniebird: *hi*
redsoxnumber1: *didn't c u at the tailgating party or football game*
marniebird: *that's cuz i wasn't there*
redsoxnumber1: *where were u?*
marniebird: *at home*
redsoxnumber1: *why?*
marniebird: *shouldn't u b out with dane or something?*
redsoxnumber1: *no, that guy is a chump*
marniebird: *LOL, u really think so?*
redsoxnumber1: *found out at the party that he doesn't like baseball, not a real man in my book*
marniebird: *ha! good point*
redsoxnumber1: *so why didn't u go out 2night?*
marniebird: *i dunno, i guess i thought i'd feel better after the SC meeting, but i don't*
redsoxnumber1: *how do u feel then?*
marniebird: *guilty*
redsoxnumber1: *for what? not kissing me again or not asking me to homecoming? ;-)*
marniebird: *just when i thought u were human*
redsoxnumber1: *i was teasing. anyway, i have a date*
marniebird: *poor girl*

redsoxnumber1: *so u feel guilty?*
marniebird: *i shouldn't b talking 2 u about this*
redsoxnumber1: *who else is there 2 talk 2?*
marniebird: *u made 2 good points in < 5 mins*
redsoxnumber1: *that's not all i can do, heh heh*
marniebird: *stop being SLEAZY!*
redsoxnumber1: *hard habit 2 break, go on talk*
marniebird: *i just feel really horrible about . . . how i treated nola*
redsoxnumber1: *because u and LL aren't friends anymore?*
marniebird: *not just that. i want to take responsibility, i was very careless with our friendship and boy did i get burned*
redsoxnumber1: *so what r u going 2 do?*
marniebird: *i want 2 say sorry but i doubt she'll forgive me*
redsoxnumber1: *NJ is still really mad at u, can tell just from eng class*
marniebird: *ugh, i know*
redsoxnumber1: *listen, the guys r here 2 watch sportscenter, so i have 2 go, but here's a lesson i learned from baseball*
marniebird: *?*
redsoxnumber1: *it ain't over til it's over*
marniebird: *tx for the yogi berra quote, how inspiring*
redsoxnumber1: *anytime ☺*
marniebird: *ttyl*
redsoxnumber1: *bye*

Chapter 24

At four o'clock on Saturday afternoon, most girls in the Poughkeepsie region were lying on their beds with their chins cradled in their hands, staring at their Homecoming dresses, which were hanging on the door of their closets. Nola James was one of those girls, too. However, she was probably the only one staring at her beautiful frock through blurry, tear-filled eyes.

Matt had left town yesterday after school, and he'd refused to let anyone treat his departure as a ceremonious event, with the exception of Boogie Bowl, that is. So now all Nola could think about was how she'd looked at Matt out of the window of her bus and waved at him as it drove away, and how not more than a minute later, she'd gotten a text message from Matt that said, DON'T CRY MISS JAMES. I'LL C U SOON, PROMISE.

Nola grabbed another tissue out of the daisy-decorated Kleenex box and blew her nose hard. After she balled it up, she carelessly threw it on the floor with the rest of the used tissues. Then she got up and shuffled over to where her lovely black dress was draped on a satin-covered hanger and touched the soft fabric. Nola sniffled and sucked in a shallow breath. How was she going to psych herself up enough to go to the Homecoming dance with Evan?

There was a knock on her bedroom door as it was opened a crack.

"Hey, Nola," a voice murmured from in the hallway.

It was Ian, of course. He always had such piss-poor timing, which is why Nola abhorred the idea of him being around to mess with her head hours before the dance.

"What is it?" Nola rubbed her eyes with her palms and then ran her hands through her tangled brown hair.

"You have a phone call." Ian opened the door a little farther and popped his head in.

Nola had turned off her cell earlier today because she didn't want anyone to disturb her while she was mourning the loss of the love of her life. Obviously whoever wanted to track her down was resourceful enough to contact her through her parents' landline. Maybe it was urgent. Maybe it was Matt!

"Who is it?" Nola asked.

"Evan Sanders," Ian replied. "He said it's important."

"Okay, I'll be right down."

Ian stared at her quizzically before making a quiet exit.

Nola bounded down the steps and into the living room, where Dennis and Dylan were playing with a Sega game, thankfully without screaming and pummeling each other (in real life, that is). Ian took a seat on the couch while Nola perched herself on the arm and picked up the cordless phone off the receiver on the side table.

"Hello," she said.

"Hi, Nola," Evan mumbled softly. In fact, his voice was so low, Nola could barely hear him.

"Evan? Are you okay?" Nola was definitely worried, especially when he groaned in pain.

"No, I'm not," Evan said. "I've been calling your cell all morning but I haven't been able to reach you. I had to look up your folks' number in the phone book."

Nola winced. She couldn't tell Evan why she'd shut her phone off, especially when he sounded as though he were being disemboweled. "Sorry about that. What's wrong?"

Evan moaned again. "Well, I went to that new French fine-dining restaurant last night for dinner. I kind of wanted to try out a few dishes, so I could make sure tonight was perfect."

Nola smiled. Leave it to Evan to do something that conscientious. "That's really sweet of you, Ev."

For some reason, Nola's eyes drifted over to Ian, who was pretending to read one of Dylan's comics but was obviously listening in on her phone call. So Nola wandered into the kitchen, where her mother and father were all gussied up and doing some last-minute tasks before leaving for their fund-raiser.

"Well, I'm afraid that . . . I've got . . . ugh . . . really, *really* bad food poisoning," Evan said, groaning in agony.

"That's terrible. Are you going to be all right?"

"I will, but not by tonight. I'm so sorry, Nola."

"Oh." Nola felt a twinge of disappointment. Sure, she'd been anxious about going to the dance with Evan when she didn't like him like he liked her. But that didn't mean that she didn't want to go *at all*. Also, Evan had gone through a lot of trouble to make this evening special. She felt bad for him, too.

Evan coughed a bit. "I feel awful about letting you down. Hopefully you'll allow me to make it up to you when I'm back on my feet."

"Sure." Nola took a seat at the kitchen table and sighed. "Feel better soon."

"Thanks," Evan said sadly. "Good-bye, Nola."

"Bye."

Nola hung up the phone, leaned forward, and rested her forehead on her arms. Then she felt a hand rustle her hair.

"What's up, kiddo?" her father asked.

Nola lifted her head up a little and looked at him. Her dad was the spitting image of an older, less buff Daniel Craig in his black tuxedo. "Evan has food poisoning. He won't be able to take me to the Homecoming dance."

Instantly Dr. James appeared at her husband's side. She was stunning in a Vera Wang red ball gown and matching silk wrap. "Oh, sweetie, that's horrible. Maybe I have something upstairs that might help him. I could do a quick house call!"

"No, Mom," Nola said, taking her mother's hand and giving it a squeeze. "But thanks for the offer."

Mr. James glanced at his grinning wife, who nodded as though she could read his mind. Then he glanced back at his daughter and smirked. "We've got a better idea."

Nola gazed at her parents curiously. What were they up to?

"Ian!" her father shouted. "Could you come here for a minute, please?"

Oh, god, Dad. Don't don't don't don't DON'T!!!

Ian strolled into the kitchen, looking rather forlorn, like Nola. "Yes, Mr. James?"

"There's been a change in plans," Nola's dad said, undoing his bow tie and unbuttoning his collar.

Wait! Waaaaaiiiiiit!!!

"Nola's date to the Homecoming dance is sick and won't be able to escort her. And instead of going to the fund-raiser, Mr. James and I will be watching the boys tonight," Nola's mother explained.

"Oh, so I guess you won't be needing me then," Ian said.

"Actually, we do need you, son." Nola's father slapped Ian on the back, a friendly gesture that sent Ian staggering forward a few feet.

"Ian, would you be kind enough to take Nola to the dance?" Nola's mother said, her smile bright.

Nola's heart dove into her stomach. Going to the dance with Ian would be a bigger disaster than global warming.

Ian seemed to think so, too. His eyes were about to leap out of their sockets. "Uh . . . um . . . I'd like to, but I don't have anything to wear."

Nola's dad put his arm around Ian and gave him a shake. "I've got a suit upstairs that would *suit* you just fine. Ha!"

“Wow, that was hysterical, Mr. James,” Ian said, his face pale.

“Please, Ian? We’d hate for Nola to miss the dance. She has such a pretty dress upstairs and was really looking forward to wearing it,” Nola’s mom pleaded while fiddling with her strand of Blue Nile pearls.

“Well . . . uh . . . okay. If it means something to Nola, then I’ll do it,” Ian said, casting his eyes on Nola’s reddening face.

What did he just say?!

Nola was positive that Ian was going to refuse. She never in a million years would have expected him to say yes. Actually, it wasn’t just a yes. It was an “if it means something to Nola.” Which was an entirely different answer altogether.

Nola covered her face with her hands and tried to sort this out in her brain. Maybe she just imagined the conversation she and Ian had about how they were supposed to remain businesslike. No “fraternizing with the boss’s little girl” was how Ian had put it. Well, wasn’t agreeing to take her to a semiformal dance in her father’s suit fraternizing multiplied by a hundred million? This didn’t make any sense!

“That’s great, Ian. Thank you!” Nola’s mother enthused. She yanked Nola’s hands away from her face and smiled at Nola lovingly. “I’ll help you get ready.”

Ready for what? Nola thought.

But when she glanced over at Ian, who was grinning at her tenderly, she wasn't sure if she wanted to find out.

The first five minutes of the ride over to Poughkeepsie Central in Ian's BMW were the most uncomfortable of Nola's life. And considering what had occurred over the last couple of hours, that was saying a lot.

Ian looked remarkable, if not spectacular, in her dad's navy blue suit and it was almost impossible for Nola *not* to stare at him. On top of that, Ian was fidgeting with Mr. James's burgundy tie so much that Nola was worried he might accidentally strangle himself or crash his car into a tree.

Nola was having a fidget-fit, too. She kept opening and closing her black beaded purse as though she had OCD. Which is quite normal for a young girl on her way to her first semiformal dance with *her brothers' babysitter*!

As the car paused at a red light, Nola rubbed her temples with her fingers and took a cleansing breath. Maybe the evening wouldn't turn out so bad. Perhaps it wouldn't be weird to slow-dance with a college guy in front of the whole school.

"Sooooo," Ian said as he anxiously tugged at his shirt collar. "This is really creepy, isn't it?"

Nola let out a nervous laugh. "Uh-huh. Sure is."

The light turned green. Ian shook his head and pressed his foot on the gas. "I should have said no to your parents. I don't know what I was thinking."

"My theory is you were just taking pity on me." Nola grinned a bit, hoping to lighten the mood.

"That's the thing, Nola. I wasn't." Ian's eyes were focused on the road, but somehow she could tell there was distress clouding them.

"What do you mean?"

Ian let out an exasperated sigh. "I have to pull over."

Nola gripped the edge of her seat as the car lurched to the left and came to a stop on the shoulder of the road.

"Sorry, I just can't drive and talk about this at the same time," Ian explained as he turned off the car.

Nola gulped hard.

"I'm just going to say a bunch of stuff and I don't want you to interrupt, okay?" Ian turned toward Nola and rubbed the back of his neck.

Nola had guessed right. Ian's gleaming eyes were dim, and although he still looked smoking hot, he also appeared quite troubled.

"I won't," she replied, tucking her hair behind her ears.

"We have a big problem here," Ian began. "You see, I *wanted* to say yes when your folks asked me to take you to the dance. I *wanted* to spend time with you when I was supposed to be watching your brothers. I *wanted* to kiss you that night in your room. And right now, I *want* to tell you how incredible you look in that gorgeous dress you're wearing."

Nola dug her nails into the seat's upholstery.

"I know you think I'm an insensitive jerk most of the time, but . . . I behave like a thirteen-year-old boy around girls I *like*," Ian said, shifting his gaze to the dashboard. "And therein lies the big problem. I'm seventeen, Nola. I'm not in a position to be feeling this way or *act* on my feelings. Do you understand what I'm saying?"

Nola understood perfectly what Ian was saying — he was into her, just like Iris and Matt had suggested! However, it also seemed like Ian was saying something that sounded like a veiled good-bye.

"I do understand, but how is the problem going to go away?" Nola murmured.

Ian's eyes met Nola's again. "I think you know there's only one solution. I have to find another job."

Nola's emotions were all over the map. She felt freaked out by Ian's admission and yet kind of stoked that he was attracted to her. She was relieved to hear that Ian was going to quit being the family manny and yet upset that once he did, she'd probably never see him again.

"Sorry about all this," Ian muttered.

"I'm sorry, too," Nola replied.

Ian attempted to smile. "Don't say you're sorry. You didn't do anything except be yourself, and there's absolutely nothing wrong with that."

Nola was unsure of what to say so she simply grinned back.

"Is it okay if I just drop you off at the dance?" Ian asked as he restarted the car.

"Yeah, sure," Nola said nicely.

"I wish I could take you, but I'm trying to be the bigger person here," Ian added.

Once the car was in motion again, Nola marveled at how this evening had turned out. Nothing had gone as expected, yet she'd weathered the storm quite well. In fact, she'd made it through the chaos without breaking out into stress-induced hives, which was astounding. Nola was actually proud of herself. Still, the experience felt kind of hollow, because she couldn't share it with Marnie.

All of a sudden, Ian's last words echoed in Nola's mind — "I'm trying to be the bigger person." Throughout her combat with Marnie, Nola had also been fighting a war inside herself. She'd felt as though reaching out to her ex-friend and being the bigger person was a sign of weakness and stupidity. But here Ian was, doing the responsible and mature thing, and Nola respected him for it. Maybe she even admired him, too.

Then Nola remembered that Marnie had been ordered by Lizette and her underlings not to show up at the dance. Which meant that Marnie was probably still at home.

"We just need to make one pit stop," Nola blurted as she pointed out the window. "Go that way!"

"Oh no," Ian mumbled under his breath, obviously not happy. Even so, he turned the steering wheel abruptly and changed course, just like Nola wanted.

Chapter 25

"So, how do I look?" Erin asked as she descended the stairway and waltzed into the living room, interrupting Marnie and her mom as they played the board game edition of *Are You Smarter than a 5th Grader?* (Thankfully, Marnie was. At least after the third round of questions.)

"Oh, sweetheart. You're absolutely breathtaking!" Mrs. Fitzpatrick chirped and clapped her hands together. "Don't you think so, Marnie?"

Marnie sighed heavily. Erin could have entered the room wearing a tacky acid-washed denim catsuit and looked as though she belonged on the cover of *Harper's Bazaar*. Her sister knew that, too, which made her all the more unlikable. Whatever sympathy Marnie had mustered up for Erin yesterday night had evaporated when she woke Marnie up this morning by blasting Marnie's iDeck, which she hadn't even bothered asking permission to borrow.

"Well, are you going to compliment me or what?" Erin nudged Marnie with the tip of her glittery silver shoes.

Marnie eyed her sister from all possible angles. There was no denying that Erin was looking spectacularly gorgeous tonight. Her hair was lifted back in a soft twist, so you couldn't miss her dazzling face. The crushed velvet criss-cross halter dress she was wearing hugged her in all the right places. Everyone at the Homecoming dance would surely throw rose petals at Erin's feet and bow in submission to her ethereal beauty.

Suckers.

"Erin, you are the incarnation of —" Marnie racked her brain for a vocabulary word that would go over her sister's head. "Maleficent!"

"Uh . . . thanks. I think so, too," Erin said, obviously trying to mask her confusion with a plastic smile.

Marnie giggled. Tonight was getting off to a good start. She was smarter than a fifth grader *and* had just tricked Erin into calling herself evil. Not bad.

Suddenly, Marnie felt a pinch near her elbow. When she turned and saw her mother's icy glare, she realized that her mom hadn't forgotten the meaning of the word *maleficent* since she learned it in high school. Now Marnie was worried that she might get sent to her room without the pizza dinner that was on the way from Gino's.

Not good at all.

However, when the doorbell rang a minute or two later, Marnie's mom hadn't gone ballistic on her.

(Phew.) Pepperoni-and-sausage pizza was most likely going to be the highlight of Marnie's evening. Sad but definitely true.

"I'll get it," Marnie said, leaping off the couch and breezing by Erin so fast she almost knocked her sister on her sequin-covered ass.

While Erin squealed something inaudible, Marnie rolled her eyes and grabbed her mom's purse off the coat hook in the hallway. As Marnie counted out a stack of ones, she tried to forget how close she was to throttling Erin within an inch of her life. Another day together and that just might happen. In fact, Marnie was slightly relieved that she wasn't going to be anywhere near Erin tonight. And so what if she missed the dance? She had pizza. She had a board game inspired by Jeff Foxworthy.

God, who am I kidding?

With a stack of dollar bills clenched tightly in one hand, Marnie flicked on the porch light and thrust open the door with lukewarm anticipation. The Gino's delivery guy handed over the tantalizing pizza after Marnie gave him enough money for the bill and a tip. Then he trotted down the porch stairs and hopped back in his van.

Marnie brought the square pizza box up to her nose, closed her eyes, and sniffed it like a bloodhound would. The aroma of the sausage made Marnie forget about missing Homecoming for a brief moment, but when she opened her eyes and saw a coupon for a free game at Hoe Bowl taped to the pizza box, she realized that she was missing something much more important.

It was the last Saturday of the month. If it had been July instead of October, Marnie would be at Hoe Bowl with Nola, engaged in their traditional bowling competition. Marnie's lower lip quivered and her eyes became teary as she recalled the time Nola accidentally squirted mustard all over Marnie's jeans instead of her hot dog, and the night Nola gave Marnie six practice frames because her aim was really off.

These and countless other memories swarmed Marnie so fiercely that all she could do was walk into the kitchen, set the pizza box down on the stove, and then grab her jacket from the wall rack in the hallway. Regardless of what Weston had said about Nola being really mad at her, Marnie had to apologize and try to make things right.

"Mom, I'm going out for a while," she shouted as she shoved her arms through her coat sleeves.

"What about the pizza?" her mom yelled back.

"I'm not hungry," Marnie replied.

"Where are you going?" Mrs. Fitzpatrick asked.

Marnie swallowed hard. "To Nola's."

"*What?*" her mom and Erin said in unison.

"I don't have time to explain. I shouldn't be too long," Marnie said, opening the front door.

As soon as she locked the door behind her, Marnie reminded herself that Nola might have left for the Homecoming dance already. Once she turned around, Marnie found out she was right.

Sort of.

There stood her ex-friend Nola.

Marnie froze for a second, wondering what Nola was doing there, all gussied up in the stunning black cocktailesque dress Nola had showed her at the Galleria. Marnie could tell Nola was nervous. There was a light red streak forming underneath her chin. The familiarity of that sight made Marnie smile.

"Hi, Marnie," Nola muttered.

"Hey, Nola," Marnie replied. "Is everything okay?"

Nola wrapped her dark silky shawl around her bare arms. "Oh, um . . . yeah. I'm fine."

"Good." Marnie gazed at Nola, hoping that this wasn't a trick. "I'm surprised to see you."

"I know," Nola said, smirking. "I'm surprised that I made Ian drive me over here."

"Ian?" Marnie looked behind Nola and didn't see anyone else.

Nola reached to her left and yanked a suit-clad Ian by the arm and into view. "Here he is."

Marnie put her hand over her mouth. From the miserable expression on Ian's face, he seemed more like a hostage than a Homecoming date. But then something occurred to Marnie.

"Wait, I thought Evan was your date," she said.

"He got sick and I'm supposed to be the stand-in," Ian grumbled.

"But he's resigning. Isn't that right, Ian?" Nola said with a half grin, like she'd just revealed a private joke between them.

"Yes, fortunately," Ian said, grinning back. "Which is what brings us here."

Marnie was so baffled, all she could say was, "Huh?"

Nola went on to explain but then the red patch below her chin turned fuchsia and she just clammed up. Ian gave her a pat on the back for encouragement and after a brief, awkward moment, Nola was able to get the words out. "Well, since Ian is dropping me off at the dance, I figured we could give you a lift, too, you know, if you wanted to go."

Marnie's heart nearly combusted into a zillion pieces. After all the BS that had gone down between them since their brutal, cataclysmic fight, Nola was essentially here to extend an olive branch to Marnie on the most important night of their lives. Marnie was more than aware that she didn't truly deserve Nola's generosity, but as tears streamed down her cheeks, she made a silent vow that she'd cherish this second chance with Nola. That is, if friendship is what Nola was truly offering. Perhaps she was just on Marnie's doorstep out of pity.

There was only one way to find out.

"Nola . . . I —" Marnie gasped for air as she tried to talk while crying. "I'll only come if . . . I can go with my best friend."

Nola looked stricken. "What did you say?"

"I'll only come if I can go with my *best friend,*" Marnie repeated, her voice cracking.

A skeptical-looking Nola stood very still.

Marnie threw her arms around Nola and hugged her tightly. "Oh, Nola. I was on my way to your house so I could tell you how *sorry* I am. I never should have lent Lizette your bracelet, or blown you off all those times, or . . . or —" Marnie coughed. "Or had my birthday party at Lizette's house. I feel soooo bad. Do you think you can forgive me?"

Nola put her arms around Marnie and sniffled into her ear. "I think so. But" — Nola pulled back and stared Marnie down — "I have to know. Do you only want to be friends again just because . . . Lizette dismissed you?"

Marnie shook her head. "No, Nola. I want to be friends again because . . . I need you."

Nola looked down at her feet. Obviously she was having trouble believing Marnie, and Marnie could understand why.

"I know it's going to take a while for you to trust me again," Marnie said, wiping tears off her cheeks. "But I'll do everything I can to earn it back."

When Nola lifted her head up, Marnie was relieved to see a small smile form on her face. "First things first. You have to hurry up and find something to wear."

Marnie grinned a little. "I'll need your help, though."

"Since when do you need my fashion advice?" Nola mumbled.

"Since now," Marnie said, grinning even more.

"Excuse me," Ian interrupted. "What am I supposed to do while you two get ready?"

Marnie and Nola looked at each other knowingly.

"I have an idea." Marnie unlocked the door and opened it. "Erin! Can you come here for a minute?"

"I thought you were going to Nola's!" Erin screamed from the living room.

"Just. Come. HERE!" Marnie screeched.

"Who's Erin?" Ian asked Nola worriedly.

"Marnie's older sister," Nola said, smirking.

As if on cue, Erin appeared in the doorway, looking rather irritated. "*What?*" she snapped.

Marnie rolled her eyes. "I have to ask you a favor."

Erin let out a sarcastic snicker. "Go ahead."

"Can I borrow one of your dresses for the Homecoming dance?" Marnie prayed her sister would come through for her now when the stakes were high.

Erin's eyebrows arched in surprise. "I guess. Who are you going with?"

Nola stepped out from behind Marnie and waved. "Hey, Erin."

"Well, this ought to be interesting." Erin chortled.

Even though Marnie knew Erin would make fun of her later, she didn't particularly care. She was just thankful Erin didn't say no.

"Thanks, sis. I really appreciate it."

"Yeah, yeah," Erin said with a half grin.

Marnie turned around and grabbed Ian by the tie, pulling him forward so he stumbled in front of Erin. "Now, could you entertain Ian while Nola helps me get ready?"

The moment Erin laid eyes on Ian and his stellar suit, her demeanor went from bitchy former Homecoming queen to swooning college girl. Marnie and Nola glanced at each other again, but this time they held in their laughter.

"Sure," Erin said, licking her lips.

"Great," Marnie said. "Come on, Nola."

Marnie skimmed past Erin and galloped up the stairs with Nola close behind her. Then she threw open the door to Erin's room and dove into her sister's closet.

"Do you think Ian will be okay talking to Erin?" Marnie asked as she rummaged around for a dress.

"Actually, I think they're made for each other," Nola joked.

Marnie saw a shimmering piece of red fabric and grabbed it off the hanger. Then she held it up to herself and jumped in front of Nola, who was sitting on Erin's bed, opening and closing her purse anxiously. Marnie couldn't ignore the shroud of tension and weirdness that surrounded them, but she told herself that if she was loyal to Nola, the shroud would eventually be lifted. All they needed was time.

"Well, what do you think of this?" Marnie asked.

There was a long awkward pause.

"You're going to look sensational in that." Nola's smile was weak, but what she'd just said made up for it.

Marnie's heart swelled with hope. "Thanks, Nola. And I know it will look great with a certain bracelet of mine."

Chapter 26

As Nola stood on the edge of the dance floor, admiring the silver streamers hanging from the ceiling and the deep purple balloons scattered around the gymnasium, she wondered what was keeping Marnie. Once Ian had left them off in front of the school, Marnie told Nola that she needed to make a quick trip to the bathroom so she could "check her face paint." But that was nearly ten minutes ago, and since then, Nola had glued herself to this spot and clung to her black beaded purse as though it could save her from impending disaster.

While her fellow students were getting their groove on to a Good Charlotte song, Nola tugged at the bodice of her exquisite black dress and tried to give herself some extra breathing room. Nola's eyes scanned the growing crowd for any hint of Marnie, but she was nowhere to be found. Immediately, the needle on Nola's worry-o-meter struck the fiery red "You asked for it!" zone. Nola shook her head with self-loathing. What if reconciling with Marnie and bringing her to Homecoming had been a gigantic mistake?

Sure, the girls had hugged it out after Marnie's tearful apology, but that didn't necessarily mean they could pick up their friendship where they left off. While it had felt really good to let her guard down and allow Marnie back into her life, Nola was already skeptical of her newly reinstated friend's mysterious whereabouts. What if on the way to the bathroom Marnie had decided to ditch Nola again and skip off to some crazy, swinging-from-the-Tiffany-chandeliers shindig that the Almighty Lizette Levin was throwing? Then Nola would be stranded here all night with absolutely no one to talk to or dance with, looking like a total reject.

Nola glanced at the clock on the wall and watched another minute tick by. The palms of her hands were slick and sweaty.

Where is *she?*

"I must say, Mrs. Billingsworth, you look stunning."

Suddenly, dull throbbing pains attacked all the joints of Nola's body. Which was not surprising, considering that the Vice President of Dirtbaggery was in close range.

Nola wanted to take her purse and slam it against the cocky smirk that was most likely affixed to Dane's face, but instead she just grumbled, "Whatever."

Dane circled around her like a rattlesnake. But when Nola got a good look at him, Dane was every bit as dapper as (although she hated to admit it) a celebrity attending a movie premiere. His dark gray pinstriped suit didn't seem the slightest bit investment-bankerish, especially because he wore a plum-colored shirt without a tie.

As Dane's eyes visually groped Nola from her hair to the slinky straps on her shoes, she swallowed hard. Forget about waiting for Marnie. She had to split — NOW.

"If you'll excuse me," Nola said through clenched teeth.

When Nola began to walk away, Dane blocked her path, just as he had in front of Marnie's house more than a week ago. "Hold up a sec. I want to dance with you."

"Well, I don't want to dance with you, okay?" Nola darted to Dane's left but he stepped to the side just as quickly. She lunged to her right and Dane matched her once more.

"You know, if you'd just put your arms around me, we'd be dancing already," Dane said, chuckling.

"I'm not going near you. Can't you get that through your thick skull?" Nola fumed.

Dane flipped up the collar of his jacket and grinned slyly. "That's a shame. I thought you and I could have a good time together." Dane leaned over and ran his hand up Nola's arm. "And I bet all my friends that you'd be an even better kisser than Marnie. Why can't we go somewhere private and find out?"

Completely horrified, Nola recoiled so fast, she almost gave herself whiplash. But as she jerked away from Dane, Nola plowed straight into Marnie, who had applied some shimmer powder on her collar bone and had redone her eye makeup in that sexy-as-hell smoky way that only professional cosmetologists are able to get right. However, Marnie's dumbfounded expression indicated that she had heard at least some of the disgusting things Dane had just said.

Dane didn't miss a beat, though. He surveyed Marnie in her gorgeous shoulder-baring red sateen strapless dress and her patent-leather black peep-toe shoes and his tongue practically started wagging. "Wow, Marnie. You are the prettiest —"

"Oh, shut up, Dane." Marnie cut him off, almost lazily. "I think I've heard enough crap coming out of your mouth."

Nola smiled. Maybe patching things up with Marnie wasn't a mistake.

"What did I say that was so bad?" Dane asked.

"Are you so clueless that you can't see you were sexually harassing my friend?" Marnie shoved Dane in the shoulders with both hands.

Nola's eyes grew wide. She never thought she'd see Marnie do something that aggressive.

"You're just jealous, that's all. And honestly, your outburst is only making Nola look hotter," Dane said smugly.

Marnie shoved Dane again, but this time she did it hard enough that he almost lost his footing.

"I'm not jealous of Nola. I'm pissed at myself," Marnie growled. "I can't believe that I fell for your act. But at least now I see you for the scum-wad Nola always knew you were."

Dane glanced over to Nola, who angrily crossed her arms in front of her chest and sneered. "A scum-wad, huh?"

"A *giant* scum-wad," Nola replied.

Dane shrugged. "Well, in that case, I guess it wouldn't surprise either of you if this scum-wad talks to Principal Baxter on Monday and tells him that there was a miscount of the votes for freshman class treasurer."

Nola saw Marnie flinch and knew something had just gone terribly wrong.

"What miscount?" All of a sudden, Marnie appeared flustered instead of bold and courageous.

Dane let out an obnoxious laugh. "Remember when I said I had friends in high places who fixed the election for you? Well, I *wasn't* kidding."

Both Nola and Marnie were silent. Time seemed to stand still as the song in the background changed to a slow R&B jam from Chris Brown. As Dane stood there, all superior and self-righteous, Nola looked at Marnie and saw how devastated she was. This sleaze had no right to mess with her!

Now it was Nola's turn to go off.

"Don't even think about threatening Marnie, Dane," Nola barked, pointing a finger in his face. "If you so much as even go within twenty yards of Principal Baxter's office, I will see to it that you spend the rest of your high school existence wishing you'd never met me."

"I highly doubt that," Dane said before his attention was caught by a sultry-looking Mini Jada, who was waving him onto the dance floor. He responded by rubbing his hands together in anticipation. "Later, ladies. Duty calls."

And with that, Dane Harris slithered away.

Nola let out a furious groan. "Oh, my god, he is . . . so . . . freaking . . . *PUTRID*!"

Then something unexpected happened. Marnie laughed.

"'Putrid'? That's the best you could come up with?" she asked with a wide smile.

Nola felt a part inside of her shift gears, kind of like when she would ride her bike and the terrain would change from rocky to flat. Then she could fly along with no trouble at all.

"'Putrid' is a good word!" she said brightly.

"Yeah, if you're British and seventy years old," Marnie joked.

"Just you wait. One day, a Major will turn *putrid* into the next catchphrase and you'll be sorry you picked on me."

Marnie sighed a little bit, obviously aware that Nola was still concerned about Marnie's level of loyalty. She put her arm around Nola, and Nola noticed how good her handmade bracelet looked on Marnie's wrist. Then she cleared her throat and in her best scum-wad voice, she said, "I highly doubt that," and winked.

Nola wrapped her arm around Marnie and doubled over with laughter. "That was awesome!"

"No, *you* were awesome!" Marnie said through a heavy stream of giggles. "Thanks for sticking up for me like that."

Nola had to admit, she felt so awesome in the thrill of this moment, she thought she might be invincible. Sticking up for Marnie and herself the way she just had was something she'd always been too scared to do. But when the chips were down, that fear had receded instead of overpowering her.

Amazing.

"Well, you stood up for me, too," Nola said, wiping tears of happiness from her eyes.

Marnie leaned her head against Nola's, like she used to do when they were in kindergarten. "I guess we have an interesting Monday ahead of us, huh?"

Marnie had just said *us*. Nola felt relieved to hear that word. It was as though everything was starting to get back on track. Actually, now that Nola thought about it, perhaps they were on a *better* track than before.

So Nola called Marnie's squeeze and raised her a full-on hug. "Yeah, we do. But we're going to face it together."

Chapter 27

"I love this DJ!" Marnie shouted above the loud *boom-boom-boom* of the bass line to "Mr. Brightside" by The Killers. She and Nola had set up camp near the refreshments table, where other classmates who didn't have dates were sipping on punch and nibbling on chocolate chip cookies that had been brought in special from The Pastry Garden bakery.

When she had been tight with Lizette, Marnie never would have hung out back here with the crew of The Young and the Dateless, fearing what her socially cut-throat friends might think. But now she didn't care one bit. Marnie was reminded of how much fun she had with Nola when her friend was being her klutzy, sarcastic, hive-handicapped self.

"What? I can't hear you!" Nola screamed back.

Make that deaf, too.

"I said, I LOVE THIS DJ!" Marnie yelled again.

Nola threw her head back in frustration. "WHAT DID YOU SAY?!"

Marnie laughed and decided that spelling it out with charades was probably the best way to get her point across. She and Nola always used to play this game on rainy days when they were in grammar school. Marnie pointed to herself, which was a sign for the first word. Then she made a heart shape with her hands to indicate the second word. Next Marnie pretended to put on a pair of headphones and started air-scratching a make-believe vinyl record.

"I got it! You love this DJ!" Nola said, practically jumping up and down.

"Yes!" Marnie raised her arms in a victory pose.

"It's good to know that some things never change," Nola said as the music died down.

Marnie smiled, even though she knew that she and Nola weren't the same people they used to be. Nola had clearly found an inner strength — Marnie didn't need to take care of Nola like she had in the past. In Marnie's case, she had been cut down to size in a way that made her awfully vulnerable. She could already feel herself needing Nola more than she had before, and that was scary territory for her, especially now that Dane was also on the anti-Marnie warpath.

Had her ex been bluffing about the election being fixed so Marnie would sweat? Or had he really gotten his cronies to falsify votes? Erin had been able to pull a bunch of strings to get Marnie nominated for freshman class Homecoming queen, so it was quite possible that Dane had done something similar to ensure Marnie's treasurer win.

Regardless, trouble was surely ahead for Marnie, and she hadn't even run into Lizette or Brynne yet tonight. But as Nola had said earlier, at least Marnie wouldn't have to face any of it by herself. Friendship didn't get any truer than that.

Once the DJ announced he was taking a break, Nola applauded. "I think I'm going to congratulate him on rupturing my eardrums."

Marnie giggled. "That's a great idea. Then you should ask him to play your favorite song."

"Do you really think he has the theme to *Hannah Montana*?" Nola asked.

"Of course, 'Best of Both Worlds' is a classic," Marnie said, fluffing up the bottom of her dress a little. "Maybe you could even hunt Matt down and dance with him!"

Nola's grin vanished and a somber frown appeared in its place. "Matt . . . um . . . moved away yesterday."

"Oh, my god. *Really?*" Marnie's mouth dropped open.

Nola twirled a strand of her brown hair around her finger as her eyes became teary. "Yeah. I'm kind of freaked, Marn. I don't know what I'm going to do without him."

Marnie shook her head as a shot of guilt pierced her heart. Here Nola had been going through her first boy crisis and Marnie had had no idea. She was so out of the loop when it came to Nola's life, she worried that no matter what she did going forward, she wouldn't be able to make up for missing out on so much.

Even so, Marnie was going to do everything she could. And she was going to start now.

"Attention, everyone! Last year's Homecoming queen is about to announce this year's winners!"

Or maybe I'll start later.

Marnie turned around and saw Erin vamping on stage with a microphone in her hands and a tiara pinned to her head. As Marnie had predicted, a hush came over the crowd and everyone stared as if hypnotized at her strikingly beautiful older sister. And truth be told, even Marnie was mesmerized by Erin's radiance.

"But first the nominees must form a group in front," Erin said, flashing a brilliant smile.

Marnie's stomach felt as though it had been poked repeatedly with a fire stoker. Did Erin just say that she had to stand in the front of the gymnasium and act gracious while Lizette, Brynne, and Grier accosted her with dirty looks?

"Freshman class nominees for Homecoming queen, please step forward," Erin said, indicating with an outstretched hand where she wanted the Homecoming court to assemble.

Marnie took a deep breath and tried to calm herself, but she was close to hyperventilating. But then she felt a tap on her shoulder. Marnie glanced to her right and saw Nola there, smiling genuinely.

"Go get 'em, Marn," she said, and rubbed Marnie's back affectionately.

Marnie grinned. Perhaps it wasn't the end of the world that she and Nola had kind of traded places. It was actually nice to be able to lean on Nola for support for once, and as she walked through the throngs of people gathered together to watch the Homecoming crowning ceremony, Marnie tried to focus on what really mattered. Regardless of what was about to happen, she'd always have her self-respect to cling to.

Since Marnie had been at the back of the room to begin with, she was the last one to arrive in front of the stage. Lizette, Brynne, and Grier were all there, waiting for her to join them. The Almighty Lizette Levin didn't disappoint with her attire. She was decked out in an electric-blue spaghetti-strapped bubble minidress, dangling rhinestone earrings, and her "sick" pair of black motorcycle boots. Grier's and Brynne's outfits were a bit more sedate. The Gap-toothed Demon actually looked demure in a long mauve satin dress, while Grier's small pixielike figure was accentuated by a short rose-colored Betsey Johnson original.

As soon as her eyes met Brynne's devious glare, Marnie could feel her legs begin to wobble. And the feeling only got worse when she cast her gaze on Lizette, who looked through Marnie as though she were transparent. Grier was surprisingly sunny, though, probably because she was thrilled to be nominated. So Marnie stood on the end near Grier, where it was safest.

"Now, would the freshman class nominees for king please come forward," Erin announced, her voice reverberating like an echo in a canyon.

Marnie wrung her hands nervously as she watched Weston lead the pack. Wearing a dark gray sport coat and a shiny burgundy tie, Weston had stayed true to his Red Sox colors. When he passed by Marnie, he gave her a little wink, which made Marnie laugh in spite of herself. Like it or not, Weston was actually getting under her skin again.

However, there was no way Weston could top the boy who trailed behind him.

Sawyer Lee, the big kahuna on Marnie's All-Time Crush List.

Dressed in his signature cargo shorts, a long-sleeved button-down shirt, a funky bow tie, and his favorite red Vans, Sawyer smiled at Marnie as though she hadn't rejected him more than once. Her pulse went berserk when his midnight eyes settled on her.

Sawyer paused in front of Marnie and held out his hand. Thinking of how he had tackled Jeremy Atwood, Marnie grinned at Sawyer, took his hand in hers, and squeezed. "Good luck," was all she could think of to say.

Sawyer squeezed back and leaned in so he could whisper something to Marnie. "Meet me in the home ec room after this."

Marnie nodded, her heart somersaulting like an aspiring Olympic gymnast.

Sawyer stepped to the side and joined his fellow nominees as Marnie looked straight ahead, refusing to return the glacial stares she could feel from Brynne's direction.

And then Nola made everything easier. This formerly shy friend of hers had somehow slipped through the masses and took a position just a few feet away from Marnie. When Nola waved to her excitedly, Marnie couldn't feel the freezing chill of negativity circling around her anymore.

"Ladies and gentlemen, it is a pleasure and a thrill for me to announce the Homecoming freshman class king and queen!" Erin proclaimed gleefully.

Marnie kept her eyes on Nola, who was crossing her fingers and most likely her toes.

"Give it up for Lizette Levin and Weston Briggs!" Erin shrieked.

Marnie wasn't surprised that either of them won, but she didn't expect to get queasy when she'd heard their names joined together as if they were a couple.

A roar of approval erupted from the crowd as Brynne and Grier got into a group hug with Lizette. Weston celebrated by chest bumping with each member of his Homecoming posse.

"Congratulations, you two," Erin said cheerily. "I'd also like to extend special thanks to my little sister, whose freshman class fund-raiser contributed the most financial resources to the Homecoming committee. Well done, Marnie Fitzpatrick!"

The audience burst into another round of applause and Marnie gasped loudly. First of all, Erin had just been uncharacteristically sweet to her — in public, no less! Secondly, Marnie's car wash hadn't raised *any* funds! Was Marnie unknowingly in the center of one preposterous joke?

"Hope you don't mind, but I talked my dad into making a large donation to our meager cause."

Marnie whipped her head around and saw Weston, mugging at her as though a camera crew were filming the two of them for a reality show called *Can You Believe Your Creep of an Ex-Boyfriend Is Actually a Nice Guy?* She was so shocked by what had just happened, she couldn't move a muscle. And beyond that shock was also the stunning realization that Weston had just one-upped Sawyer in the good deeds department.

Was the world about to blow up?

"I think the response you are looking for is 'thank you,'" Weston said, his eyes gleaming.

"Thank you," she managed.

"Now gimme a hot car-wash kiss."

"Fat. Chance."

"Are you going to dance with me or what?" a voice whined from behind Weston.

Weston turned around so he and Marnie could get a full-on view of Poughkeepsie Central's new freshman class Homecoming queen.

Marnie took one look at the snooty snarl on Lizette's face and immediately became incensed. "Didn't anyone teach you that it's *rude* to interrupt people's conversations?"

"I wasn't *talking* to you." Lizette adjusted the tiara that had been pinned to her hair and sneered.

Brynne must have heard Lizette blow a dog whistle because she scampered right over and got in Marnie's face. "I thought I told you not to show up tonight."

Marnie glanced at Weston, who seemed mighty happy to have front-row seats to an all-girl brawl.

"You know what, Lizette?" Marnie stared fiercely into Brynne's eyes. "One day, this no-good witch is going to turn on *you* and I hope I'm there to see it."

Lizette tugged on Brynne's dress and Brynne instantly backed off. Then Lizette took Weston by the hand. "I'm sure you'll be sitting in the *cheap seats*."

Marnie gnashed her teeth. "*Screw you.*"

Lizette rolled her eyes and dragged Weston onto the dance floor, leaving Brynne and Marnie to their own devices. Marnie peered over at Nola, who was staring at her with concern. It was enough to strengthen Marnie's resolve and she didn't back down.

"So how was your in-school suspension?" Marnie asked cheerily. "I hope you got a lot of soul-searching done."

"You're going to pay, Marnie. Just you wait," Brynne threatened.

Marnie sneered at Brynne with all her might and held out a steady hand. "Look how much I'm shaking," she said sarcastically.

With that, Brynne growled and skirted away to join the other runners-up for king and queen. Marnie glanced to where the boys had been standing in line and saw that Sawyer was no longer in their company. In the midst of her duel with Lizette and Brynne, she'd somehow forgotten all about him.

Yikes! I've got to get to the home ec room! PDQ!

But first, she had to explain to her best friend that she had to duck out of the dance for a little while.

As Marnie dashed over to Nola, a tingle of anxiety went up her spine. What if Nola became upset at Marnie for leaving her behind to rendezvous with Sawyer? Marnie hated to think of their relationship being that fragile, but then again, if it was, she was to blame.

Marnie made a vow then and there to *always* take Nola's feelings into account. If Nola seemed the least bit annoyed or irritated, Marnie wouldn't leave the dance to meet Sawyer. That was that.

Oh, god. Here goes.

Marnie gulped hard and hoped she'd say all the right words, but the only thing that would come out was, "I lost."

"I saw," Nola said. "Along with everyone else in the entire school."

"Yeah, right." Marnie chomped her lower lip nervously. *Okay, just say it or you're going to draw blood.* "Listen, Nol. Sawyer Lee just asked me to meet him in the home ec room."

Nola's eyes grew to the size of a half-dollar. And not in a good way. "He did?"

Marnie paused and inhaled deeply. It was totally reasonable for Nola to be nervous — Marnie had let her down so much lately. "I won't go if it'll upset you. It's our first night back together as friends and I wouldn't even think of ruining that. So be honest. If you want me to stay, I will. And I won't be mad."

Nola's worried expression slowly transformed into a genuine but small smile. "Don't be long, okay?"

Marnie hugged her friend tightly. "You're the best, Nol."

"Save the mushy stuff for Sawyer," Nola joked.

When Marnie finally arrived at the home ec room minutes later, she was drenched with so much perspiration it was as though she had just gone on one of her morning runs. But she wasn't going to waste another second freshening up.

Marnie could see the room was dark, so she opened the door quietly and snuck in. She was about to turn on the light, when suddenly a match was struck and Sawyer Lee's smiling face was illuminated with a golden glow.

"I'm glad you could make it, Marnie," he said in a near whisper. "And I'm glad you patched things up with Nola."

Wow. Whoa. And oh, my god.

Sawyer lit a small votive candle and set it on a desk. Then he walked over to Marnie and pulled his green iPod out of the pocket of his cargo shorts. Marnie's heart raced as Sawyer tucked a strand of her hair behind her ear. Then he put one earbud in his left ear and offered Marnie the other one.

"What's going on?" Marnie didn't really care, but she still had to know what all this was about.

Sawyer stroked Marnie's warm cheek with his fingers. "Well, I knew you wouldn't dance with me out there because a certain someone might see us, so I . . . improvised."

Marnie was so choked up, her voice box was rendered useless, but she did manage to put the earbud in. Once Sawyer wrapped his arms around her and she laid her head on his chest, Marnie was certain she'd never speak again. Luckily, she regained her voice after their candlelit slow dance, which lasted for the first four songs on Sawyer's Secret Homecoming Dance playlist.

And what Marnie said was: "Let's do this for real."

Chapter 28

At first Nola wasn't sure what possessed her to say yes when Carl Franciscovich, a fellow student in her advanced freshman physics class, had asked her to dance. She didn't know Carl particularly well, nor did she want to get to know him. Carl was, in a word, peculiar. (As in constantly-wears-large-trifocal-glasses-and-has-a-problem-with-dry-scalp kind of peculiar.) Still, Nola found it hard to dismiss Carl when he'd somehow summoned up the courage to leave his cluster of Mathletes and approach her as she lingered near the refreshments table, consuming her fifth cup of fruit punch.

However, as she and Carl swayed back and forth to a Justin Timberlake slow jam, Nola realized why she hadn't shot Carl down. She actually related to the guy. On the first day of school, the thought of talking to *anyone* other than Marnie had Nola in a panic. While Nola still had a lot of battles left to fight in regards to her shyness, she hadn't suffered a nervous breakdown because Marnie had gone off with Sawyer instead of hanging out with her (although there was a shot of insecurity, understandably). She just wasn't as self-conscious as she had been in early September. The same could probably be said for her peculiar dance partner, too, and Nola suspected he felt a bit empowered tonight, like she did.

When the song ended and Carl thanked her for the dance, he scampered over to his friends with a silly grin on his face. Nola got a small kick out of seeing how happy Carl looked, but as soon as the DJ cranked out a familiar melancholy tune, her heart went into convulsions.

She'd heard this song for the very first time while standing on a rooftop and staring at her soul mate.

By the second word of the opening verse, every single memory Nola had of Matthew Thomas Heatherly flooded her brain. She was so overwhelmed that she stood motionless in the spot where Carl had left her on the dance floor. Boys and girls had coupled off all around her, gazing into each other's eyes as though they were truly lovesick. But Nola knew that they had no idea what it really meant to feel that way. They didn't have a clue how much it hurt and they didn't know that the hurt never lets go. It was almost . . . paralyzing.

Nola closed her eyes and tried to get ahold of herself. All she had to do was put one foot in front of the other until she reached the parking lot, where she could come to her senses in the crisp night air. Nola willed her strappy sandals to detach from the ground beneath her, but she couldn't move.

What happens now that we've gone this far?
Do we believe in wishes made on falling stars?

As Nola listened, her eyes still shut tight, she could almost hear Matt's voice.

"I'm really glad this DJ takes requests."

Nola's eyes sprang open, her heart suddenly beating a hundred miles a minute.

Matt was right there in the flesh, within hugging distance, as quirky and funny and gorgeous as he had been the first time she'd talked to him in homeroom. Even so, Nola still couldn't move. In fact, she was certain all her bodily functions had shut down.

This has to be a dream!

Matt let out a sigh that was as soft as the faded black T-shirt he was wearing. "It's so good to see you, Nol."

Lips. Teeth. Tongue. MOVE!

"How . . . I mean, why . . . um . . . *what are you doing here*?" Nola stammered.

Matt smiled. "I took a Greyhound bus back to Poughkeepsie because I forgot to give you something."

Nola was so flabbergasted, she combined "huh?" and "what?" into one meaningless word.

"Whauh?"

"A going-away present," Matt explained as he held

out his hand. In his palm was a tiny blue velvet box with a red ribbon.

"But *you're* the one who went away," Nola said, her hand trembling mercilessly as she reached out for it.

"I know," Matt replied, his cheeks turning pink. "And I didn't realize that I wanted you to have this until I was already gone."

Nola took the gift from Matt and undid the silk ribbon carefully. Then she flipped open the box and saw . . . a guitar pick.

Oooookaaaaay.

Nola looked up at Matt confusedly and said, "Thanks, it's . . . great."

"Somehow I have the feeling that you don't see the significance of my present," Matt said, laughing.

"I guess I don't," Nola said.

Matt closed in a little more as their song reached the third chorus. "Remember how I couldn't tell you the name of this band?"

"Yeah, I do." Nola was afraid that if she blinked Matt might disappear.

"Well, the band . . . is me."

"*You?*"

"I wrote the song and played all the instruments and sang and recorded it at my dad's studio," Matt gushed excitedly. "And I used that pick for my guitar solo, which is my absolute best, hands down."

Nola didn't want him to say anything else. She just wanted him in her arms.

"Anyway, this pick has become kind of a symbol of hope for me, and on my way up to Binghamton, I couldn't stop thinking about you. So I decided that . . . I wanted you to have it with you at all times, since I can't be," Matt said, closing in even more.

Now they were in lip-lock range.

Nola's emotions had her tilting back on her heels, although all her instincts were telling her to lean forward. If Matt just thought of her as strictly a friend, would he have traveled all this way to give her something that was this important and say something that insanely sweet to her? Her head was pounding so hard, she was frightfully dizzy.

Thankfully, she was still able to dig deep and speak from her soul.

"I don't think I'll cherish anything more."

Matt reached out with both arms and pulled Nola in for the most precious hug she'd ever received. "I know I'm an ass for realizing all of this yesterday, and Evan is going to kill me once he recovers, but . . . I am crazy about you, Miss James."

Nola's chin was on Matt's shoulder and he had

whispered this right into her ear so there was no mistaking it for a mixed signal.

Matt Heatherly was crazy about *her*!

But what was Nola supposed to do now?! She'd waited for this moment forever and now that it was here, she was feeling that dreaded paralyzed sensation again.

Over Matt's shoulder, Nola could see Marnie and Sawyer Lee on the sidelines of the dance floor. Marnie was leaping in the air like a cheerleader on a caffeine binge while Sawyer laughed in amusement. Obviously, she was psyched to see Nola in Matt's arms. However, Marnie calmed down long enough to answer Nola's telepathic plea for help by mouthing a quick set of instructions for her best friend again and again.

Kiss him! Kiss him. KISS HIM!

As wonderfully romantic as the situation was, Nola couldn't stop herself from laughing.

"What's so funny, beautiful girl in the amazing dress?" Matt asked while tracing his fingertips gently along Nola's bare back.

Nola pulled away from Matt a little, so she could gaze upon the face that would always stir her heart. Then without deliberating about what to say or how to say it or what to do or who was watching (i.e., the entire school), Nola breathed in the scent of Matt's favorite brand of Axe, closed her eyes, and pressed her lips against his.

As they kissed, Nola was completely transfixed by the experience, which felt fantastically new yet completely relaxed and intimate. Matt tasted like hot cocoa and oatmeal. His mouth moved tenderly against hers; his hands moved down and clutched at her waist. Nola felt like any minute now she might go delirious with joy, and then she realized, she already had.

Matt slowly released Nola from their kiss and gently leaned his forehead against hers. "So that was . . . really . . . *wow.*"

"Are you blushing?" Nola giggled.

"Please, rock stars don't blush," Matt said with a wink.

"I'm supposed to believe you're a rock star now, Mr. Ego?" Nola laughed.

Matt pulled back so he could stare into Nola's eyes. "Actually, I just want you to believe in me."

Nola's smile stretched across her face for miles. "I do."

Matt grinned as his song came to an end and Madonna's "Music" blasted through the DJ's sound system. "Yes!" he exclaimed and threw his hands in the air.

Nola started laughing so hard, she was blinded by tears.

"You guys mind if we mosh with you?" a boy's voice said.

Nola's watery eyes darted to the left. Marnie and Sawyer were standing together, hand in hand, ignoring all the stares they were receiving from Lizette, Brynne, and everyone else on the dance floor.

"Can you really *mosh* to Madonna?" Nola asked.

"Sure you can. Watch." Matt bounced up and down to the rhythm while Sawyer quickly mimicked Matt's every move. Within seconds, both guys were shoving each other playfully as Marnie and Nola looked on in hysterics.

Marnie put her arm around Nola and yanked her close so she could yell, "I can't believe you kissed him!" in her ear.

"I'm *so* glad I did," Nola shouted, sounding elated. "And I can't wait to kiss him again!"

Marnie stepped back and gave Nola a look of mock shock. "Since when did you start talking to me about kissing boys?"

Nola's smile was all aglow as she hip-checked Marnie. "Since now."

"Well, what do you say, Nol? Want to show the inept mongrels at Poughkeepsie Central our sassy dance moves?" Marnie did a couple of twirls and then held out her hand.

Nola grinned as she looked at Marnie's bracelet and locked fingers with her friend.

"I'm in."

Acknowledgments

I applaud the Wonder Women at Scholastic/Point, who always do right by my books: Aimee Friedman, my friend–itor and a veritable wellspring of pizzazz; Abigail McAden, head honcho of all things awesome; the indefatigable Morgan Matson; and publicity guru Sheila-Marie Everett. A standing ovation also goes out to my family, friends, and fans of the IN OR OUT series. I've never worked this hard in my entire life, and I couldn't have done it without all of you.

Take a sneak peek at *The Year My Sister Got Lucky*, the brand-new novel about sisters, best friends, city life, and country life by *New York Times* bestselling author Aimee Friedman.

I lean against an ancient-looking gum-ball machine and check out the other customers. A young ponytailed mother is pushing a baby in a stroller and examining the jars of homemade strained pears; a grandpa type in a fisherman cap is picking through a mound of shiny apples, and a blond guy with his back to me, who looks to be about Michaela's age, is studying a rack of Hanes underwear.

I'm a little embarrassed for him.

"Katie, want to pick out some fudge?" Michaela asks, waving me over to the counter. Mr. Hemming is ringing up the Scotch tape and babbling about the weather while Mrs. Hemming is asking Michaela if she's ever hiked up Mount Elephant — whatever *that* is. "We can take it home to surprise Mom and Dad," my sister adds brightly, but the look in her eyes screams: *Please come save me from this crazy old couple.*

I hurriedly join Michaela just as Underwear Boy makes his way toward the register. He has a couple packets of white boxers under his arm, and my face grows hot even before I notice how good-looking he is.

He's tall and well built, with broad shoulders that strain against his orange T-shirt. His hair is a curly, shaggy mop that falls into eyes so pale, pale blue they're almost translucent — but in a good way. He has a high forehead, and a straight nose, and a firm chin with a dimple in it. I don't want to stare, so I glance at my shoes, the heat from my face sliding down into my neck. From the corner of my eye, I see Michaela pay and step aside to make room for Underwear Boy. He doesn't seem the slightest bit flustered about buying boxers out in the open.

"Hello, Anders," Mr. Hemming booms, placing the boxers in a bag. "How are your mother's tomatoes doing?"

Anders? I mouth to Michaela. What kind of a name is that? My sister shrugs back at me.

Anders mutters something about the tomatoes doing fine and then turns around with swift, natural grace that makes me realize he's an athlete. He could also be a dancer, but that's very doubtful.

My heart clutches as Anders stands still for a second and glances from me to Michaela. The corner of his mouth lifts, like he wants to either smile or say something. I'm not sure what to do, so I glance at Michaela for assistance, and to my astonishment, my sister is looking right back at Anders and not even trying to hide it. Her mouth is in a half smile, too. What's *wrong* with her?

Anders lifts his chin at us — possibly his way of saying hello — then saunters out of the store, letting the door bang behind him.

"That Anders Swensen," Mrs. Hemming clucks from behind the counter. "He was such a nice boy when he was younger, always smiling and saying 'please' and 'thank you,' but ever since he was named quarterback — well, Lord help me for saying this, but he's become a bit . . ." Mrs. Hemming pauses like she's about to curse. "Rude," she finally whispers, her brown eyes enormous behind her glasses.

"Too handsome for his own good is what I say," Mr. Hemming speaks up gruffly, counting the change in the register.

"It really is a shame," Mrs. Hemming prattles on, obviously pleased to have an audience. "I hear he's breaking girls' hearts right and left at the high school." At this, Mrs. Hemming pauses and her bow-shaped lips part. "My heavens," she adds, sizing up me and Michaela. "You girls are starting at the high school, aren't you? You know it's right down at the edge of Main Street, don't you now?"

I shake my head, overwhelmed, while Michaela nods.

"Be careful, is all I have to say." Mrs. Hemming drops her voice to a scandalized whisper as the young mother approaches the counter. "Kids today, they can be plenty cruel, especially to newcomers, if you catch my drift."

Oh, *please*. I try not to roll my eyes. You haven't known mean until you've dealt with city kids: uptown trust-fund girls with salon-straightened hair, five-hundred-dollar boots, and tongues like knives and hard-core punk boys wearing studded dog collars who steal your MetroCard out of your back pocket. I've seen it all. And in junior high, though I never rolled with the A-list, I was never shunned, either — and besides, there was always ballet school, where my *real* life happened anyway.

"Thanks for the heads-up," Michaela tells Mrs. Hemming, putting her hand on my shoulder to indicate we should escape while we can. The Hemmings call to us that our family must come over for dinner sometime, and then Michaela and I are safe.

"What were you doing?" I ask my sister, a little breathless.

"I'm sorry!" Michaela says, swinging the bag from Hemming's Goods. "I wanted to get out of there sooner, but those two didn't stop talking —"

"Not the Hemmings." We're nearing the end of Main Street and I see it up ahead, like a hulking brick giant: the high school. "That guy. Anders or whatever. You were *staring* at him! While he was buying boxers." I'm scandalized.

Michaela's face flushes briefly. "What's wrong with

looking?" she asks. "Didn't you think he was exceptionally hot?"

"I guess." I watch my feet as they step over the cracks in the sidewalk. I'm not used to debating the hotness of real-live boys with my sister.

By now we've reached the high school, so we come to a stop and gaze up at our future. Carved into the white stone above the entrance are the words FIR LAKE HIGH SCHOOL, ESTABLISHED 1955. The building is sprawling, with a green lawn and flag pole out front, and what look like endless sports fields in the back. Like everything else about Fir Lake so far, it's movie-perfect and picturesque; a world away from the urban plainness of LaGuardia High School. I can practically see the blonde pigtailed girls jumping into convertibles with their pom-poms — until I remember it's *not* 1955. And I know that a pretty building can just be a facade for real ugliness inside. I think of what Mrs. Hemmings said, and for one frightening second, wonder if the country bumpkins at Fir Lake High *might* give city kids a run for their meanness money.

"So how bad do you think it's gonna be?" I ask Michaela, feeling a stab of anxiety.

My sister pauses before answering. "I have a good feeling about this year, Katie. I can't explain it, but I do."

And just like that, I believe her. We *can* handle anything, Michaela and I — even a deer in our backyard and arrogant football players and sandals over socks. I grin at Michaela, and she grins back. Look out Fir Lake High School, here come the dancing Wilder sisters.

To Do List: Read all the Point books!

By Aimee Friedman

- ❑ South Beach
- ❑ French Kiss
- ❑ Hollywood Hills
- ❑ The Year My Sister Got Lucky

❑ **Airhead**
By Meg Cabot

❑ **Suite Scarlett**
By Maureen Johnson

❑ **Love in the Corner Pocket**
By Marlene Perez

❑ **Hotlanta**
By Denene Millner and Mitzi Miller

Summer Boys series by Hailey Abbott

- ❑ Summer Boys
- ❑ Next Summer
- ❑ After Summer
- ❑ Last Summer

In or Out series by Claudia Gabel

- ❑ In or Out
- ❑ Loves Me, Loves Me Not
- ❑ Sweet and Vicious
- ❑ Friends Close, Enemies Closer

❑ **Orange Is the New Pink**
By Nina Malkin

Making a Splash series by Jade Parker

- ❑ Robyn
- ❑ Caitlin
- ❑ Whitney

Once Upon a Prom series by Jeanine Le Ny

- ❑ Dream
- ❑ Dress
- ❑ Date

PNTLST3